GRANNY BURNS RUBBER

A SECRET AGENT GRANNY MYSTERY BOOK 10

HARPER LIN

This is a work of fiction. Names, characters, organizations, places, events, and incidents are either products of the author's imagination or are used fictitiously.

GRANNY BURNS RUBBER

Copyright © 2021 by Harper Lin.

All rights reserved.

ISBN: 978-1-987859-85-0

www.harperlin.com

ONE

I'm beginning to think there's something wrong with me.

Murders keep happening wherever I go. I can't go to a book club meeting, a Sunday drive, or even on a school field trip with my grandson without someone dropping dead. Once a body even dropped into my shopping cart.

It's becoming a frightening trend, and one that's made my retirement in the sleepy little suburb of Cheerville anything but sleepy.

But I thought that I could at least help a friend plan a wedding without a body turning up.

Silly me.

I'm Barbara Gold. Age: 71. Height: 5'5". Eyes: blue. Hair: gray. Weight: none of your business.

Specialties: Undercover surveillance, small arms, chemical weapons, Middle Eastern and Latin American politics. Current status: Retired CIA agent, widow, and grandmother.

Addendum to current status: wondering how I inadvertently got a wedding planner drowned in a mass of wedding cake.

Perhaps I should back up.

Of all the oddballs I'd met since I moved to the superficially boring town of Cheerville in order to live close to my family, none are more interesting than my friend Liz Danfrith. When we first met, we saw a lot of each other, literally. I had infiltrated a nudist colony in order to investigate one of Cheerville's endless string of untimely deaths. She had been a suspect, then had been an ally, then had become a friend.

Since exposing the case of the murdered nudist and causing a scandal from which Cheerville barely recovered, Liz and I had seen each other many times. Liz was a healthy, slim girl in her early forties (being on the wrong side of seventy, I get to call a middle-aged woman a girl) who was fit and active.

She was also an outspoken activist for nudism. The bumper stickers on her Lexus said "I brake for naked people" and "I can't bear not being bare." I skipped over that part of her personality and enjoyed her company for chats over coffee, strolls through the Cheerville Botanical Garden, and the occasional short hike.

I had only set one rule to our friendship. Clothing was not optional. It was mandatory. I'm not a nudist, or a nakedist, or a full-body suntanner, or whatever the term is these days. I'm also not a prude. Liz can do whatever she wants with her own time, but if she's in my house, I want her clothes on. Her house is governed by her rules, so she came over to mine, or we met in one of Cheerville's many clothing-mandatory cafés.

There was only one little cloud over our friendship. No, not the nudism. Instead it was her suspicious past. She claimed that she had been a forward observer in the Army, reaching the respectable rank of first lieutenant. A forward observer is positioned as close to enemy lines as possible in order to call in locations for the artillery to hit.

I didn't believe that for one minute. I can smell a cover story a mile off, having made up so many of my own over the years.

Oh, I believed that she had been in the armed forces. Perhaps she'd even been in the Army. But she knew too much about too many things to have been simply an officer with a specialized skill set. Her training was too broad. I felt convinced she had been a bit closer to enemy lines than some camouflaged observation post. I think she was actually behind enemy lines.

Much of our conversation was taken up with talking about her boyfriend, Captain Rick Dillon. He had been serving in Afghanistan (a place Liz suspiciously knew a lot about) and was just finishing up his third tour of duty. He was resigning from the force and due back within a week. They had promised each other they would get married when he returned. Liz asked me to help plan the wedding.

"I'm so excited, but there's so much to do," she enthused as we sat one afternoon at the Tick Tock Café, infamous throughout Cheerville as the noisiest place in town at every quarter hour. Every wall was covered with clocks, many of the cuckoo variety. There must have been a couple hundred of them.

"Weddings can take a lot of planning," I agreed.

"I've never been married before. Heck, with my army duties, I've hardly even *been* to any weddings before."

"Don't worry," I reassured her. "I've been to heaps of them. I'll help you out."

"Great! And, of course, you've been married yourself. What was your wedding like?"

James and I had been in the CIA together. He had proposed in a bunker as we were getting shelled by mujahideen. He got down on one knee, his fatigues dusty and blood smeared on his face, and said, "We might not get out of this alive, so I have to ask you—will you marry me?"

How can a girl say no to that?

Poor man. The Islamists attacked just then, and he had to wait through a two-hour firefight before he got his answer. Actually, I shouted "yes!" several times through that battle, but my words got drowned out by gunfire.

Neither of us being the kind to waste time, we got married at a forward base. A chaplain helicoptered in for the occasion while a trio of Special Forces girls were my bridesmaids and a brigadier general walked me down the aisle (actually a space between a wall of sandbags and a line of mortars) to give away the bride. James's best man was the battalion sniper. A buddy of his in the Air Force arranged a flyover, which turned into a bombing run against an enemy force trying to sneak up on our position.

That sort of set the tone for the rest of our marriage.

"So what was your wedding like?" Liz asked again, pulling me out of my memories.

"A quiet affair in the country. Just a few close friends."

"Ours is going to be a little different," Liz said, an impish smile growing on her face.

I looked at her askance. "It's not going to be a nudist wedding, is it?"

Liz laughed. "No! Rick's family is super conservative. They'd have a mass heart attack. No, it's going to be a military-style wedding."

"Are you going to have it on base?" I tried to remember where the nearest base was. Cheerville and the surrounding area weren't exactly national security hotspots.

"No, we're going to have it at Lakeview Park with Megaton Army Surplus doing the arrangements."

I blinked. "I've been to that army surplus shop to buy camping gear. I didn't realize they catered weddings."

"Oh, yes. They even have his and hers tanks."

"I beg your pardon?"

"We're each going to ride up on one, and when

we get married, they shoot confetti out of their guns. One's painted with blue camouflage, the other with pink."

"Doesn't sound like very effective camouflage."

"Well, it's not like we're going to be in mortal danger," Liz said.

Just then, every clock in the place rang the quarter hour. A loud *booong* reverberated through the café.

I should have taken it as an omen.

TWO

Lakeview Park was exactly what it sounded like, a lovely hundred acres of rolling hills, copses, and picnic tables with Cheerville Lake at the center.

The lake itself wasn't very big, a roughly circular body of water half a mile in diameter, but pretty enough. It had been spared any "development" thanks to being entirely owned by the municipality. The only building was an activities center, a sizeable wooden bungalow right by the lake used by various organizations and school groups. Liz and Rick had rented it for the big day, just a week away.

We had gone down to check out the venue because the wedding planner who Liz had hired to oversee the caterer, decorations, guest list, dealing with the venue, dealing with Megaton Army

Surplus, et cetera, et cetera, et cetera, was running another wedding today.

To my disappointment, this particular wedding wasn't being run by Megaton Army Surplus, so the parking lot only had a caterer's van and a couple of employees' cars—no his and hers tanks. I had to admit they had piqued my curiosity.

The actual vows for today's wedding were taking place at Cheerville Central Baptist Church (located between Cheerville Baptist Church and Cheerville Southern Baptist Church), and then the wedding party would come down here for the actual eating and drinking and dancing that most guests show up at weddings for. Especially the drinking. So we had a little while to check out the venue and talk with the wedding planner Liz had hired.

We were greeted at the door by Fiona Younger, owner of Getting Hitched Wedding Planners, a chirpy woman in business casual with the blond bob that seemed to be part of the uniform of Cheerville's female professional class. As soon as she saw us, her face lit up like we were long-lost friends reunited after years of separation.

"Hey, Liz!" she said, rushing out to greet my friend with a big hug and air kisses. She turned to me. "And you must be Liz's mother."

"Um, no. Just a friend. I'm Barbara Gold."

"So great to meet you!" she squealed, treating me to a big hug and air kisses too. "Come on in. I want to show you everything!"

The lake house had several function rooms, mostly closed and dark at the moment since the wedding party had rented the entire venue. On a corkboard by the door, I saw a schedule of events including meetings for various local clubs, a kid's birthday party, and another wedding. The place looked fully booked. Liz had been lucky to get a slot.

We passed down a hallway to a huge room on the lake side of the building. There was a floor-to-ceiling window along one wall, offering a sweeping view of the lake and the surrounding park. A few motorboats puttered around the lake, along with those bright-red plastic boats you paddle side by side with a friend. A small marina and boathouse stood on the opposite shore. Along the lakeside, a few families strolled, their children splashing in the shallows.

The view was so pleasant, it took us a moment to notice how the wedding planner and her crew had decorated the room itself. White crepe hung along the upper part of the windows. At one point was suspended a large photograph of a young man and woman arm in arm while smiling at the camera.

They looked in love. I wished them well as I thought of James. Tables and chairs filled about half of the room. To one side, an area had been cleared for a dance floor, complete with DJ booth and disco ball.

Along the center of the room, a long table groaned under the weight of a giant three-layered wedding cake, buckets of ice for the champagne that was soon to come, and a cornucopia of cakes, pies, snacks, nibbles, hors d'oeuvres, munchies, tidbits, and all the other words you use for stuff you stuff yourself with.

"Of course, this is a traditional wedding," Fiona was saying when I tuned back in to her and Liz's conversation. "Yours will have the military theme you requested. But even so, the basics are the same. Dance floor over there. The DJ can play any type of music you like. Your fiancé has already sent me his request list. Send me yours when you get the chance. Dining area over there. Open bar and full waitstaff. And, of course, the food! This is our general layout. If you have any specific requests, feel free to email me."

"It looks great," Liz said, surveying the feast.

"You haven't decided on a cake yet," Fiona said, pulling a glossy folder out of her briefcase. "Check out these samples."

Liz opened it up, moving next to me so I could see. I felt flattered. I'd planned a couple of weddings before and always appreciated being asked to share in someone's special day. Liz and I really had become close.

We flipped through the pages showing different styles of wedding cakes—two-tier, three-tier, four-tier, ones garlanded with edible flowers, ones painted in sugar with beach scenes that looked like they had been done in watercolor, even vegan and gluten-free cakes. As different as they all were, they had one thing in common—the high price. Add that to renting the venue, hiring the staff, and supplying the food, and this would be a serious expense. I felt grateful that James and I had a wedding on the cheap. We didn't even have to pay for the bombing run.

"I like this one," Liz said, pointing to an ornate three-tier cake with lots of pink frosting. I was about to point out that it hardly fit with the theme of a military wedding when she asked Fiona, "Can you make this in camouflage and the frosting look like barbed wire?"

To her credit, Fiona didn't skip a beat. "Sure! Any color you want. The cake maker is a genius. She can use spun sugar for the barbed wire."

"I've never eaten barbed wire before," I quipped.

"You'll love it," Fiona said. "Trust me."

"I'll take your word for it," I replied.

"Megaton Army Surplus sells wedding cake figures," Liz said. "I'll go pick up a bride and groom in fatigues."

I turned to her, surprised. "They sell those?"

"Sure. Haven't you ever been in their wedding supplies aisle?"

"I didn't even notice."

"So it looks all set," Fiona said. "I can have the bakery get to work on the wedding cake, and I'll chat with Megaton about the other arrangements. I'll need an initial down payment of five thousand."

I blinked. You could buy a lot of Kalashnikovs for that.

Fiona pulled a credit card machine out of her briefcase.

"Not a problem. Hold on," Liz said, reaching into her pocket.

Just as Liz pulled out her wallet, several things happened all at once.

Firstly, Liz fumbled her wallet and dropped it, causing her to bend over to retrieve it.

Secondly, there was a cracking sound from the direction of the window. I spun, as much as my knees allowed me to spin, and I saw a bullet hole.

Thirdly, the wedding planner fell face-first into the wedding cake with a splat.

I spun back to look at her and saw a growing bloodstain on her back.

Liz saw it too.

"Shooter!" she shouted, diving for the floor.

I didn't need to be told. I was diving for the floor right alongside her, although not as quickly as I would have liked.

As we hit the deck, another crack came from the direction of the window, and a second bullet hole appeared a little below the first. The bullet thudded into the far wall.

We heard the roar of a motorboat. On instinct, we rolled in opposite directions. Once I'd made it a few feet, I peeked from behind the cover of a chair and saw a small boat about two hundred yards out on the water. A masked man was at the helm of the outboard motor while a second one, gripping a pistol with a silencer, aimed at us.

"Stay down!" Liz told me. "He's going to fire again!"

Like I needed that explained to me. That's youngsplaining, a bit like mansplaining but where younger people assume older people are blithering idiots.

They never seem to realize that we're old because we've managed to survive all these years.

I kissed the carpet. A series of cracks told me he was unloading on us. I felt a spike of pain as a shard of glass cut the back of my hand.

Then the firing stopped. We heard the motor speed away.

Glancing at Liz and seeing she was unhurt, I poked my head up a little to check out what was going on with the shooters. Their boat skimmed over the water to a forested area on the far side of the lake, about a quarter mile along the shore from the marina. Nobody on shore appeared to have noticed what they were doing, thanks to the silencer.

The boat slowed as it approached the shore. The guy at the tiller headed straight for land and beached it. The two masked men leapt out and disappeared into the woods.

In shock, Liz and I got to our feet and hurried over to Fiona. I felt her neck for a pulse, but no. She was dead.

THREE

The police came quickly enough, taking our statements, bandaging my hand, and sending a squad car over to the marina, which was the only spot on the little lake where you could rent a motor-boat. Liz was visibly shaken and told the police she had no idea why anyone would kill poor Fiona Younger.

The shaken part might be true. The ignorance of the killer's motive? Not so much.

Because it seemed obvious to me that the real target had been Liz.

My friend had been standing right between Fiona and the window when she dropped her wallet. It was only pure luck that she bent over at that moment and the bullet meant for her ended up in

Fiona's back. Liz was sufficiently versed in ballistics and reaction times to know that.

But she decided to play dumb. Why?

As she went through her story, she kept glancing at me, as if she knew I suspected she wasn't telling the whole truth. I maintained a poker face.

I needed to get her alone and grill her. I had nearly been shot, too, so it was almost as much my problem as it was hers.

Actually, it was equally my problem. Liz was a friend, and the definition of "friend" is that you share their problems.

Assuming she'd share with me.

I really needed to have a long heart-to-heart with her away from Cheerville's bumbling police department.

That would have to wait because who came into the reception hall but Cheerville Chief of Police Arnold Grimal, his belly straining at his dress shirt like the prow of some very poorly designed ship. The kind that sinks on its maiden voyage. His slack face had a put-upon look to it. Solving murders was well above his skill level. He took one look at me, groaned and muttered something unprintable, followed by "Of course she's here."

He proceeded to ask Liz and me all the same

questions as his officers then got on the radio for a while, speaking to his patrol cars. With the help of some neighboring police forces, they had set up a net around town, blocking off all roads. But none of the cops had stopped a vehicle with two men in it. They had stopped and questioned everyone, and the only people they had seen were locals who were known to them. No strangers, no suspicious characters. They had searched every vehicle and had come up with no weapons.

So either the killers had gotten away before the dragnet was put in place, or they were still hiding somewhere in Cheerville.

Either option seemed possible. Checking Google Earth on my phone, I saw a road passed right by the stretch of woods where the killers had beached their rental boat. All they had to do was bolt through about two hundred yards of woodland to the road, where they could have left their getaway car on the shoulder or perhaps had a third person waiting for them. It would have only been a matter of minutes before they were on the highway and headed away from Cheerville.

Or they could have stayed in town, waiting for their next chance.

"So did the staff at the marina give a good

description of who rented the boat?" I asked Grimal when he got off the radio.

He stared at me. "What?"

"Did the staff at the marina give a good description of who rented the boat?" I asked in slow, clear English. Any time I tried to speak to him at anything above a third-grade level, he'd stare at me like I was speaking Swahili.

I actually do speak some Swahili. You need to if you want to make deals with East African arms dealers in exchange for their giving up the location of terror cells. But I digress.

Grimal waved a dismissive hand. "Hardly anything. Middle-aged white guy. About six foot. Wore a hat and sunglasses, so they couldn't get any more of a description. The guy had to provide picture ID, a driver's license, but we ran it and it's a fake. They didn't even notice the second perp. The people at the marina are a bunch of idiots."

"Takes one to know one," I muttered.

"I beg your pardon?"

"Nothing."

Grimal turned to Fiona's body, which was still draped over the table, her face buried in the wedding cake. The second and third layer leaned over her like the famous tower in Pisa. The bride and groom figures had fallen off the top and lay snapped in half on the floor.

Poor Mr. and Mrs. So-and-so. Their wedding was ruined.

Well, at least they weren't here to see it.

A loud honking of several cars sounded outside. Grimal got on his radio.

"What's that?" he demanded.

An officer's voice crackled over the air. "The wedding party, sir. They just showed up."

Grimal turned beet red. "You didn't go to the church to warn them off?"

"You didn't tell us to, sir."

Grimal groaned and rolled his eyes. "Well, I'm telling you now."

"You want me to go to the church?"

"No, intercept the wedding party! Get rid of them!"

He put his radio down and shook his head. "I'm surrounded by idiots."

"I know the feeling," I said.

Grimal glared at me for a moment then turned to Liz. "Do you have any idea why someone would want to kill your wedding planner?"

Liz shrugged. "Unsatisfying honeymoon?"

Grimal turned redder. "I'm serious."

"I have no idea. I never imagined someone would want to kill her."

That was the first thing she had said since the murder that I fully believed.

Grimal hitched up his pants. His belly made it so they were constantly slipping. "Well, ladies. I'll take it from here. How about the two of you go home?"

"All right," Liz said, trembling a little, her voice wavering. "I think I need some time to recover."

"I'll be in touch if I need to speak with you again," Grimal said gently.

I put a reassuring arm around her, and we left the reception room. We passed through the hallway connecting to the front entrance. We could see the flashing lights of a parked police car coming through the open doorway, but for a moment we were alone.

As soon as we got out of sight of the police chief, her back straightened, and her voice came out level, businesslike.

"That bullet was meant for me," she said.

"I know."

She stopped. We turned to face each other. She gave me an appraising look.

"I know you know," she said.

"And I know you know that I know," I replied. "Now that we know so much about each other, care to enlighten me as to who would want to take you out with a professional hit?"

Liz sighed, leaning against the wall, her eyes taking on a faraway look.

"I... it's not your problem," she said.

"That's not how friendship works."

"If they came for me once, they'll come for me again."

"I've been shot at before," I told her.

"I know. You even got hit a couple of times. In the gut and in the thigh."

"How did you... oh, right." My clothing usually hid that wound. Of course, she'd seen me without clothing.

"Look, I can't pull you into this."

"That bullet came as close to me as it did to you. And then when they opened up, they were spraying the whole room. They didn't mind if I got taken down."

There was also the possibility that first shot had really been meant for me, and the guy was just a bad shot, or glare from the sunlight on the window had made our images unclear. Maybe. The hit seemed too professional for them to make such a mistake. I couldn't dismiss the possibility, however.

In the end, it didn't really matter. I'd investigate this until I got the gunmen.

Liz paused for a long moment. "I'm going to need to get a motel. Can you do me a favor? Could you get a room under your name? I'll pay you back."

I waved away this idea. "You're staying with me. It will be safer if we stick together."

"I can't—"

"You can. Go out to your car and wait for me. I'll be along in a minute."

"What are you going to do?"

"I need to have a chat with the so-called law in this town."

Liz headed out to the parking lot while I turned back to the function hall.

When I got there, I saw a sight that nearly made me lose my sanity.

Grimal was eating some of the cake. He didn't even have the decency to eat from one of the upper layers. Oh no, he was actually eating from the very same layer into which the wedding planner had landed. He was eating from the other side, not actually around her head, but the mere fact that he was eating it at all made me want to find a nice, cozy mental safe space and stay there for about fifty-four years.

"I think I'm going to be sick." I moaned, leaning against the doorway.

Grimal looked up, fork halfway to mouth, a guilty expression on his saggy face, a bit of frosting on his chin.

"I'm hungry. I have to keep my sugar levels up to keep my brain sharp."

"Your brain is never sharp, and it's only ten in the morning. Didn't you have breakfast?"

"Yeah, but now it's time for second breakfast."

"I thought only hobbits had second breakfast."

"Call it brunch, then."

"I call it unutterably horrifying. Isn't this interfering with a crime scene?"

"The CSI guys already took pictures."

"Ugh." I turned away as he took another forkful.

"So who's trying to kill you?" Grimal asked.

He knew a bit about my past. Once when he tried to interfere with my investigation into one of Cheerville's endless string of murders, he got a good talking-to by the director of the CIA. Now he walked on eggshells around me, all the while hoping to embarrass me enough to drive me out of town.

He had failed every time. Hinder me? Yes. Annoy me? Yes. Irritate me? Oh, yes. And now he was sickening me.

But his question brought up a quandary. Grimal, being Grimal, would only see the obvious solution, that the bullet had been meant for me. He wouldn't suspect Liz at all, even though she had told him she had been standing right behind Fiona and was only saved by suddenly bending over. Grimal was blind to that. I had been in the room; therefore I must be mixed up in it somehow.

Should I enlighten him?

Had better not. Until I had a good heart-to-heart with Liz, I didn't know what I was dealing with. Getting Grimal involved would only muddy the waters. If I needed him, I could always bring him in later. He was accustomed to being late to every investigation.

"I don't know who shot through that window," I said in all honesty. "I'll be looking into it."

"Now, wait a minute. I'm the law around here."

I tut-tutted in my best Disapproving Grand-mother tone. "Really, young man. Your investigative skills are no better than your table manners."

I left him sputtering over his stolen cake. As I walked out of the wedding venue, there was a spring in my step. Nothing like a murder investigation to liven up a wedding.

FOUR

Liz and I sat in my living room, drinking chamomile tea as Dandelion, my tortoiseshell cat, engaged in a life-and-death struggle with Liz's shoelaces. We had been silent for a time, each lost in our own thoughts. Since Liz seemed reluctant, at last I broached the subject that was on both our minds.

"That seemed like a professional hit," I said.

"Not too professional," Liz said, taking a sip from her tea.

"True. They had a pistol, not a rifle. With a proper sniper's rifle, or even a high-end hunting rifle, they could have fired at you from the woods on the opposite shore."

"But then they wouldn't have been able to use a silencer."

"Was that important?"

"Apparently," Liz said. "They didn't want to attract attention. Nobody around the lake shore even noticed them until they grounded their boat. The small sound the silencer made couldn't be heard over the sound of the motor, and the pistol was hard to see."

I raised an eyebrow. "It was plenty clear to me."

"That's because it was pointed at you."

"True enough. Any firearm you're on the wrong end of takes on the dimensions of a cannon."

Liz grinned. "You'd know."

I took a sip from my tea and didn't reply.

Liz grew serious and went on. "Whoever did it, they wanted to keep witnesses to a minimum. A rifle would have attracted attention and would have been harder to conceal on the way in and out of the job."

"If they didn't want to attract attention, they shouldn't have hired a boat. That left witnesses."

"That's why I don't think they're full professionals. Perhaps they were in a hurry too. Maybe they only learned where I'd be at the last minute and had to improvise."

"And getting you at home in the middle of the night would be too dangerous. I presume you're a gun owner. And you probably have a nice burglar alarm. Maybe even a booby trap or two?"

Liz didn't bite. "I have a pair of Dobermans. Dandelion probably smells them. That's why she's attacking my shoes like she's a lion and my sneakers are a pair of wildebeests."

"She does that to everyone. But let's not get off track. I want to help you, Liz, and I have the resources to do so. But to help you, I need you to level with me."

"What do you mean?"

Liz put on an innocent face. It was about as convincing as the innocent face my grandson, Martin, uses when I find the cookie jar inexplicably lighter than when I left it.

Actually it was a lot more convincing than Martin's big-eyed, innocent look. She had an expert poker face. A professional poker face, one might say. But I had already suspected she was more than a simple artillery observer and decided to call her bluff.

"Professional hitmen don't go after US Army veterans," I told her.

"Semiprofessional," Liz corrected.

"And artillery observers, while highly qualified in their field, don't generally know much about assassins."

Liz got a wry smile. "Neither do retired government contractors. What did you say you did again?"

She had me there. When she had seen me in my birthday suit, she'd noticed a bullet wound a couple of inches to the left of and a little below my belly button that I'd gotten in the Sinai. I tried to explain it away as laparoscopic surgery, but I could tell she knew exactly what it was. I had another wound on my upper thigh, earned in El Salvador.

Matching Purple Hearts. They always look better in a pair.

"Never mind about me," I said. "I'm not the one who got shot at."

Liz's face darkened, and she looked out the window. "They'll try again."

"Like I said, you can stay here."

Liz shook her head. "I can't get you involved."

Involved in what? She obviously didn't want to tell me. At least she wasn't playing innocent anymore. I was starting to get somewhere.

"They nearly shot me trying to shoot you. If they knew you were going to the lakeside and when, then I'm sure they know where you live."

"I'll hide out in a motel or something."

"If you disappear, then they'll try to get you

through one of your friends, like me. It wouldn't take much sleuthing to find out who I am and where I live. Whatever their skill level, these people are obviously determined. I bet the only reason they didn't hit you at your house is because you're entrenched and have a defensive perimeter."

The military term made her look at me curiously. I gave her a little nod. I wasn't allowed to reveal my old job, but I didn't think the CIA could complain about a simple gesture, right?

"So just what kind of 'government bureaucrat' were you?" she asked.

"The kind with the skill set to help you, even if my hair is gray and I have more wrinkles than a week-old Kleenex during flu season. I don't suppose you were really a forward observer, eh?"

"I was a forward observer," she said somewhat defensively.

"A *very* forward observer. Look, Liz, you can't tell me and I can't tell you, but we can work together. Stay here with me. We'll go to your house and pick up a few things. To stay safe, call the police and tell them you remember a few details you didn't mention. Have them meet you there. The presence of a squad car will be an added deterrent to your unwelcome friends. Then we'll get rid of the cops, who—believe me—are useless anyway, and come back here."

"We might get tailed."

"I'll handle that."

A slow smile spread across Liz's face. After a second, it was reflected in mine.

"This is going to be fun," she said.

"Yes, it is," I replied.

We both laughed.

"Call the cops," I told her. "We'll drive separately to the mall and leave your car there, and then drive to your house in my car. Less of a chance they'll recognize it."

"OK."

Once Liz had ditched her car at the Cheerville Musical Mall ("Shop 'til you drop. Bippity Bop!"), we drove together to her house.

She had to give me directions. While I had been friends with her for nearly a year, I had never been to her place. I hardly found that surprising. Liz was a woman with things to hide.

She needed to hide a little less if she was going to survive to her wedding day.

"So who's after you?" I asked. Might as well be direct.

Liz sighed and looked out the window at the

quiet, leafy little town where she thought she could live a peaceful life. Fat chance. That hadn't worked for me either.

"I really don't know. I'm serious, Barbara. It could be any one of a number of people. Or groups."

"Sounds like you had an eventful career."

"Oh, yes," she said, her voice heavy.

"Could it have something to do with Rick?"

"I doubt it. They would have waited for the wedding otherwise. Rick is a grunt. A wonderful, heroic grunt, but no more of a target than any other soldier serving overseas. No, this is all on me."

"Does Rick know of your career in the... whatever you were in?"

"A little. Not much. Not much I can tell him."

"And not much you can tell me," I added. "You're going to need to think, Liz. You said you retired a couple of years ago. Assuming that's true, who would still be gunning for you?"

"It is true. I am retired. But there are plenty of people who want me dead. For purposes of revenge, mostly."

"Revenge can simmer for a long, long time. I've been on the receiving end of that more than once."

"Well, in that case, our friends in the boat could be from a dozen different organizations."

I looked at her sidelong. Was she CIA? NSA? BATF? The government had a whole alphabet soup of organizations poking sticks into hornets' nests worldwide. And sometimes their operatives got stung.

I got the impression that she wasn't holding out on me any more than her former employers required. That was a problem. If she didn't know who was after her, it would be a thousand times more difficult to track them down before they struck again.

Liz directed me to a quiet cul-de-sac. Hers was the house on the end, with a good field of view down the street for three hundred yards. A high wooden fence enclosed her backyard. I saw trees beyond, a strip of forest that she could hide in if someone attacked her house. It was as good a defensive position as you could hope for in a middle-class suburb.

A police car was parked in the street out front. An officer stood knocking on Liz's front door. We had deliberately arrived late so the cops would make it there before us. That would help scare off any potential assassins. We hoped. They had proven themselves pretty brazen already.

"I'll get rid of him," Liz said.

As we pulled into the driveway at the side of the house, I noted the little black globes of security cameras covering each corner. A long, thin wire ran from the upper floor out over the backyard, where it was secured to a high branch. At the end attached to the house, a coaxial cable ran from the wire through a hole drilled below a window and into the house.

"You're a ham radio operator."

Liz looked at me with surprise. "How did you know?"

"I know an end-fed long wire antenna when I see one."

"I like to tinker with electronics," she said evasively.

"So did James." Especially electronics that set off big explosions. "I never got into ham radio. So you like to talk around the world, eh?"

She gave me an enigmatic smile. "Lots of interesting conversations."

We took a final look around.

"The coast looks clear," she said. "Let's go."

I unzipped my purse so I'd have easy access to the 9mm pistol I kept inside. Liz and I went up to the police officer. While I scanned the area for potential threats, Liz gave the officer information about when her wedding was planned and when her fiancée was due back from Afghanistan. He dutifully wrote all this down.

"We'll make sure both of you are safe for your big day, ma'am," he said as he left.

"That was easy," Liz said.

"The police here are sleepwalkers," I told her.

We went to the front door. I'd feel much better once we were inside. With a final look over her shoulder, Liz unlocked it.

As soon as she opened the door, a huge black form leapt out and slammed into me.

FIVE

I fell back on the pavement. As I hit, I had enough of a reflex to tuck in my head so it wouldn't smack into the concrete and knock me out cold.

It still gave me a jarring impact to my back and a sharp pain akin to a three-foot-long knitting needle going down my spine and inside my right leg.

Ah, sciatica. You're like malaria, that unwelcome visitor who comes and goes unannounced, but is never far away.

But I had more to worry about than that telltale sign of aging. I was just barely holding back the growling, snapping jaws of a huge Doberman.

I had it by the neck, its fangs an inch from my face. Its muscles bunched, and I felt my arms weaken. The beast's hot breath wafted in my face as those fangs drew closer...

"Poofles! Heel!" Liz shouted.

The dog leapt off me and came to sit by Liz, who stood in the doorway, holding the collar of a second dog, who stared at me, growling.

"Are you all right?" Liz asked.

"Ouch. Um, no. He set off my sciatica."

"Bad dog!" she shouted.

Poofles whined and ducked his head.

"Inside, the both of you!"

The Dobermans retreated inside.

"You named that monster Poofles?" I said, trying to get up without moving my spine or right leg. Easier said than done.

"Poofles and Doofles. Cute names for cute animals," she said with a bright smile as she gave me a hand.

"Ouch! You and I have different definitions of the word cute."

I grabbed hold of the doorway, hoping Poofles and Doofles didn't nip off my fingertips, and painfully hauled myself into something approaching a vertical position.

"How come I didn't hear them barking when the policeman was knocking at the door?"

"I've trained them not to bark unless I'm at home," Liz said.

"So if you're away, intruders will get a nasty surprise. If you're home, you'll be alerted. Clever."

I hobbled inside with Liz's help. This was a bad development. Every now and then, this annoying ailment flared up and half crippled me for a day or three. Painkillers and careful stretching exercises helped, but nothing took it away except a session with my acupuncturist. I wasn't going to be much help to Liz in this state.

She eased me to an armchair and ran off to get some painkillers. I looked around. It seemed, at first glance, a typical living room. A nice furniture set bought at some mid-priced outlet, flat-screen TV, pictures and knickknacks on the walls and mantelpiece.

Only on second glance did I see evidence of a life interestingly lived.

A picture of the fiancé in dress uniform stood on the mantelpiece. He looked at the camera with a square-jawed smile. Next to it were several smaller photos of gun-toting Afghani tribesmen posing for the camera. Allies, at least when those photos were taken. I also noticed a native basket from the Amazon rainforest, a wooden mask covered in embroidered strips of cloth used in place of a niqab by the Bhandari tribeswomen of Pakistan and Iran, and a fist-sized chunk of concrete with spray paint on it.

Poofles and Doofles lay nearby, staring at me with animalistic hunger and rage. I knew for a fact that if Liz wasn't there, they'd have turned me into hamburger within five seconds.

There's a reason I'm a cat person.

Liz came back with a glass of water and some painkillers. I thanked her.

"Is that a piece of the Berlin Wall?"

"Yes. You have a good eye."

"They used a distinctive type of concrete. I notice it doesn't have one of those silly little verification plaques all the tourist kiosks in Berlin put on them."

"A sure sign they're fakes. This got chipped from the actual wall."

"Not by you, unless you were a child." The few remaining sections were all closely guarded as public monuments.

"No. By somebody else. I'll go pack."

Well, that was informative.

She left me with the two hellhounds. I'd take

Dandelion gnawing at my shoelaces and tearing up my upholstery any day.

Liz returned in less than two minutes carrying a large satchel.

"I think you have time to retrieve more than your bug-out bag," I told her.

"We shouldn't linger. Let me leave some food for the dogs."

"You got a gun?" I asked after her as she disappeared into the kitchen, followed by Poofles and Doofles. Animals understand human speech when they want to and ignore it when it suits their purpose. A bit like teenagers.

"A 9mm automatic. It's in the bug-out bag," she called back.

"Of course you do," I muttered. "How silly of me to ask."

I tried to shift my weight and get in a more comfortable position. My back and one leg were killing me. At least I hadn't tweaked my spine. That would have put me out of commission for days.

I heard Liz pour out a mountain of kibble, and those two monsters began to gobble it down as loudly as they had been growling a moment before. Well, at least they weren't gobbling down my entrails.

"What else do you have in your bug-out bag?" I called across the room.

"The usual stuff."

"Grenades?"

"No." She sounded disappointed.

Liz returned, grabbed the bug-out bag, and helped me to my feet. A sharp twinge went down my back and leg. I hissed in pain.

"You good to drive?" she asked.

"Maybe you should," I conceded.

"Thanks for doing this," she said, parting the curtains a little and checking outside.

"Anything for a comrade-in-arms."

She gave me a sharp look then broke into a smile.

"Let's go."

We made it to my car without getting shot or me falling down, both of which I considered accomplishments, and we headed out.

"Keep an eye out for tails," Liz said.

"Difficult when I can't turn around," I groaned.

"Do your best."

We drove for a while in silence. Liz took a circuitous route. After a few minutes, she whispered, as if to herself, "I can't even get any peace on my wedding day."

"You will," I said, giving her a sidelong look. "We'll figure it out."

By the time we made it to my house, my back felt even worse, no doubt from twisting my neck constantly to watch for pursuit.

"I hope Mr. Chong does house calls," I grumbled as we hobbled to my front door.

"Who?"

"He runs Get to the Point Acupuncture."

"Are we going to pin the murder on him?"

"Don't needle me."

"You have a sharp wit."

We entered. I tenderly lowered myself on the sofa and arranged some cushions around me.

My physical state made me feel seriously cheated by life. I have been in tip-top shape since I was a little girl. I was the best female athlete in my class all through school and university and endured the rigors of combat and espionage for decades. Now I'm worse off than many people who spent their prime years in a cubicle.

It turns out that overusing your body can be just as bad in the long run as underusing it. Maybe I should have eaten more sour cream and onion potato chips when I was younger. I love those things. You can't eat anything crunchy while waiting in ambush, though. Gives away your position.

From the couch, I directed Liz to the guest bedroom and linen closet, and once she left, I got on the phone to Mr. Chong.

"Howdy, Grandma Barb. Y'all doing good today?" Mr. Chong asked, stretching out every syllable.

Mr. Chong emigrated from China to Mississippi and did stints in Texas and South Carolina before moving to Cheerville. The only type of English he speaks is Southern, which he pronounced "suthun," with a bit of Texan thrown in.

"Hello, Mr. Chong—"

"You can call me Bubba."

"Um, all right. I've had a bit of an accident. Do you do house calls?"

"For you, ma'am, I'd walk through faa carryin' a bucket full of propane."

"You'd walk through what?"

"Faa."

"You mean fire?"

"That's what I said. Faa."

"When can you come over?"

"As fast as a hound dog chasing a T-bone."

"I presume that's fast."

"Sure thang."

I gave him directions to my house and hung up. Liz returned to the living room.

"Sorry to pry, but did you just tell someone to come over?" Liz asked.

"He can be trusted. He'd walk through faa for me."

Liz's forehead crinkled. "Huh?"

Just then my phone rang. Grimal.

"Catch them yet?" I asked.

"No," Grimal grumbled. "The dragnet isn't finding any suspicious characters. I checked the local hotels and the ones on the nearby stretch of interstate. We've followed up on a couple of the guests. None panned out."

"I think they're still in Cheerville. They could have gotten away, but they want to strike again. I think they're close. They might have taken a rental home. Have you checked those?"

"Rental homes? We're getting those next."

You are now that I've suggested it.

He hung up without even saying goodbye. Not that I minded. It made the conversation shorter.

The roar of an engine outside made Liz grab her gun from the holster hidden under her vest and run for the window.

"Is it a Trans Am with a light on the hood that goes back and forth?"

"Yes."

"That's my acupuncturist. Big *Knight Rider* fan."

Liz returned her gun to the holster. Neat little job. She wore a loose vest and had a slim holster. Not even I had spotted that she had been packing. My own gun was still in the other part of the house. I'd need to get it once Mr. Chong had fixed me up.

The doorbell rang. Liz answered it. Mr. Chong entered.

Or should I say, made an entrance.

He wore a stiff red robe with a dragon in gold brocade wrapping around his body. In his delicately manicured hands he carried a box of lacquered black wood. On his head he wore a ten-gallon hat.

"Howdy, ladies," he said, touching the brim of his hat. He turned to Liz. "I don't think I've had the pleasure. I'm Bubba. Bubba Chong."

"Um, pleased to meet you, Bubba."

"That makes two of us."

"Shall I take your hat?" Liz asked, unable to keep her eyes off the huge cowboy hat.

"I'll keep it if you don't mind, ma'am. Part of my Eastern mystique."

"Huh?"

"East Texas. Now, while I'd be happy to chew the rag with you until the cows come home, I do believe Barbara here is having a bit of an emergency."

I had already worked my way into a prone position facedown on the couch. Dandelion took that moment to leap on my back and curl herself up on my rear end.

Bubba gently picked her up and deposited her on the floor.

"There you go, little lady. Now what seems to be the trouble?" he said, probing my tender back with his fingers. "Ah, I see. Plain as pigeon poop on fresh tarmac, as the wise Confucius said once."

"That doesn't sound like Confucius," Liz said, peering out the window.

"Not the ancient philosopher. A guy I knew who worked at Galveston airport. Let's get that shirt off, Barbara, and I make that request that as a medical specialist and a gentleman."

With his help, I managed to remove my blouse without too much excruciating pain. Down to my brassiere, I lay on the couch again as he opened up the lacquered box to reveal an array of needles.

"Gah!" Liz said.

"Y'all got a problem with needles?" Bubba asked.

"They give me the heebie-jeebies."

"I didn't mean to heebie your jeebie. I do apologize."

"You might want to look away, Liz," I said.

She went pale as Bubba Chong pulled out a long needle from his box and turned away to look out the window.

Just in time to keep her from seeing him tenderly stick the needle into one of the nerve centers on my back.

The tightness in my back eased. It did not go away entirely, but the effect was immediate and noticeable. Thank God for six-thousand-year-old civilizations. They tend to pick up a handy tip or two over all that time.

He started putting more pins in my back. Those who haven't had acupuncture are probably curling their toes at the moment, but there's really nothing to it. It hardly hurts at all, and what little sensation you get from the super-thin needles is more than compensated by the loss of pain in your back or joints or wherever else your body ails you.

After about half an hour of this treatment, Liz still keeping vigil at the window, not having turned around in all that time, I rather resembled a content, pain-free porcupine.

My contentment wasn't to last long, however. I heard the sound of breaking glass from the rear of the house.

"What in tarnation was that?" Bubba Chong asked.

"Trouble," Liz replied, drawing the pistol from under her vest.

She didn't get to say anything more because just then two men burst into the living room.

SIX

Now, I don't generally go into combat without a shirt on. As inspiring as all those fantasy paintings of female warriors wearing chainmail bikinis may be (at least to adolescent boys), I've always preferred to be fully clothed when I have to kill someone.

But life-and-death situations rarely come at ideal times. In fact, they can be downright inconvenient.

So I rose from the couch in only a brassiere and slacks, looking like some latter-day Amazon and feeling deeply grateful that I could move again, ready to join in the fray.

And discovered I didn't really need to.

At least not for the moment.

The two men who rushed into the room wore identical black sweatpants, black tops, black gloves, and black ski masks. They looked like low-rent ninjas. One held the pistol with silencer, the other a hammer.

That's right, a hammer. Not a gun or a knife or a can of pepper spray or even a halberd, an actual *hammer.*

Who were these jokers?

Liz didn't waste time finding out. She fired at the one who posed the biggest threat—the guy with the gun.

Shot it right out of his hand. I was impressed.

Bubba Chong leapt up, an acupuncture needle in each hand. He looked ready to come out with one of his southern witticisms when he got rudely interrupted by Hammer Man swinging at him.

Bubba responded by poking him in the chest with a needle. Ducking another swing, he poked him again.

Hammer Man did not seem overly fazed by this treatment. It was time for me to get in on the action before I lost the best acupuncturist I've ever met.

I looked around for a handy weapon. The only thing in reach was the cat. Tempting, because if Dandelion was going to live with me for any length of time, she'd have to learn how to handle herself in combat, but I decided against it.

Bubba backed away, passing me as Hammer Man kept swinging at him.

"Stick him in a pressure point!" I told him.

"I can't. Dang cuss is moving around slicker than an oiled snake!"

Bubba backed off from another swing then poked him again.

I rushed to my purse sitting on the floor next to the couch, suddenly remembering the little can of pepper spray I kept there.

I bent over to retrieve it, not feeling a single tweak of pain thanks to the expertise of my Southern-fried friend, and retrieved the can.

The two ducked and wove around each other, Bubba poking him with the needles, Hammer Man trying to knock the acupuncturist's brains out. It was an unfair competition, but Bubba managed to dodge every swing. He certainly had the motivation to.

I shot pepper spray right into Hammer Man's face. Or at least tried.

Unfortunately, he saw it coming and ducked away. Bubba thought the guy was retreating from him and charged forward.

Right into the cloud of pepper spray.

"Augh! Is this how you say your thank-yous for relieving severe back pain?"

"Sorry!" I said, clotheslining him with one arm as I tripped him so he fell flat on his back. Not a nice thing to do, but it was the only thing I could do to keep him from getting hit by Hammer Man's next swing. He fell to the floor with a thud and an unprintable word of protest.

Now I had to look after myself. Hammer Man was coming for me.

I edged backward, grateful that Mr. Chong had managed to fix my back before I got into deadly combat. My only regret was I hadn't had a chance to get my shirt on. My nudist friend probably thought that was funny.

How was she, anyway? I had been so occupied with my own problems for the last few seconds, I hadn't given a thought to her. Very inconsiderate.

I didn't have time to check, either. Hammer Man swung at me then dodged as I tried to send a poof of pepper spray into his face. I kept my finger on the button, chasing him with a cloud of noxious gas, and was rewarded by seeing him flinch then stumble over the coffee table to land on the floor, taking some of my best china with him.

I turned to check out how Liz was doing. She and the gunman struggled with one another, the intruder wrestling with Liz's gun arm while she used her free hand to pummel him. Neither seemed to have much of an advantage.

The pistol with the silencer lay not far away. I moved over, stooped to pick it up, and stopped.

Liz's bullet had put a severe dent right above the trigger. It looked like it had bent the chamber. A couple of hairline cracks spiderwebbed away from the dent. If I tried to fire that thing, it would blow up in my hand.

I stood for a moment, uncertain. Liz and the gunman bashed against a wall, knocking down a photo of Frederick as a boy, proudly sitting on a bright-red Raleigh bicycle he had received for his tenth birthday. The picture smashed on the floor. Strangely symbolic. Frederick fell off that bike more often than he stayed on it.

The two of them toppled on the floor, rolled several feet, and knocked over a side table, smashing a snow globe Martin had given me last Christmas. Water and fake snow splashed over the combatants.

A shadow and a rushing sound just behind and to my side warned me the second intruder was back up. I jumped to the side, my heart wrenching when I realized I wasn't going to make it.

It didn't matter. He wasn't coming after me. He

rushed up, gave Liz a kick in the side, and yanked his pal to his feet.

By the time my friend had recovered from this ungentlemanly treatment, they had disappeared out the back. I peeked into the kitchen, where a door led to the garden, and found they had broken a window by the door in order to get in. That was what I had heard before their sudden entrance. They hopped over the fence and disappeared.

I hurried back to Liz and helped her up. She wiped her eyes and let out a little cough. My eyes smarted, too, as did my nostrils. My little spray-a-thon had left traces of pepper gas all over the room. I went over to a window and opened it.

Forgetting that I was topless.

Just then the Gunthers, an elderly couple a few doors down, came power walking down the sidewalk, wearing identical blue jumpsuits and headbands. They stared at me, open mouthed. I squealed and turned away, only to reveal my hedgehog back of acupuncture needles.

I retreated farther into the room, where they couldn't see me. At least they hadn't heard the shot. A 9mm isn't all that loud, and Liz had fired from inside a house with all the windows closed.

Mr. Chong sat on the floor, rubbing his swollen

eyes. It looked like he had gotten a good whiff of that pepper spray. Dandelion was nowhere to be found. With her acute sense of smell, I couldn't imagine what she thought of the whole affair.

"Are you all right, Mr. Chong?" I asked.

"My eyes feel like they're on faa!"

"I suppose there's no acupuncture cure for pepper spray. I do apologize. Liz, go get some water."

She was already coming out of the kitchen with a large glass and a sponge. It looked like she had dealt with the stuff before.

Liz started applying water to his eyes, mopping it off his cheeks with the sponge.

"Gosh darn, that smarts. Who were those damn Yankees?"

Liz and I exchanged glances. I motioned to her. It was her decision how much she wanted to reveal.

"We're not entirely sure," Liz admitted. "They're trying to kill me."

"Kill a cute little filly like you? That's downright mean. Them boys is lower than a sow's belly."

After a few minutes, Mr. Chong felt better and we managed to get him all packed up and his cowboy hat on his head.

"You better steer clear of us until this is all over," I told him.

"You ain't going to call the law?" he asked.

"Don't worry. I think it's better if we handle it."

His bloodshot eyes lit up. "Ah, you're gonna have yourselves a necktie party. Well, if you catch them varmints, invite me along. I'd love to watch 'em swing."

"You can have a front-row seat," Liz told him.

"You sure you don't need an extra six-gun at your side? I don't like seeing ladies getting hurt. Makes me hotter than an Alabama summer."

"We appreciate the offer, but it wouldn't be fair. We're not sure who's after us anyway."

"Well, if you do need my help, you got my number. I think I'll go home and fix myself a mint julep."

He left, with both of us covering his retreat from vantage points at the windows, ready to gun down anyone who tried to hurt the noblest acupuncturist Cheerville has ever seen.

After he drove off, we reconvened in my wrecked living room. Dandelion peeked out from under an armchair in the far corner, looking spooked. I knew better than to try to coax her out. She'd emerge in her own time.

"I feel terrible he got hurt," Liz said, shaking her head. "He almost got killed."

"He seemed to take it in stride."

"Too many Western movies. Did you see how fast on the draw he was with those needles? Looked like a real gunslinger. He needs to decide what accent he wants, though, John Wayne or Rhett Butler."

"He immigrated to the South then moved to Texas. It's understandable," I told her.

"What isn't understandable is how they tracked us here. We should have spotted them if they were trailing us."

"I think they know a lot more about us than we do about them. If only we had something to go on," I said, looking sadly over my ruined living room. Then I spotted the hammer lying on the floor. "Eureka!"

"You don't smell too good yourself," Liz quipped.

"Har har."

I picked it up, not bothering to handle it carefully since they had been wearing gloves and no doubt were cautious about wiping everything down before coming for us.

It looked like an ordinary claw hammer. Brand new. At the squared-off base of the handle, I noticed a price tag had been torn off. Some of the sticky stuff on the back of the tag remained adhered to the rough wood. Whoever did it hadn't been careful, and enough of the top portion remained that I could read the letters "Chee—"

"Isn't there a Cheerville Hardware on Seventh and Main?" I asked.

"I think so. I've never been there."

"Neither have I, but we're going now, and I hope they remember selling someone a hammer, because it's the only lead we have."

SEVEN

Cheerville Hardware was a stand-alone building in a small lot. It had a subdued concrete exterior with large windows in front showing off a wide variety of tools. Behind and to one side, I spotted a tall, spacious shed with different types of lumber piled in orderly rows on thick shelves. As we got out of the car, my nostrils filled with the smell of grease and sawdust.

We passed through the door, a little bell tinkling an announcement of our arrival. We saw three aisles of tools and materials. At a counter by the door stood an older man with a beer belly, thinning hair, and muscular arms.

"Good afternoon, ladies," he said.

If only.

We smiled and walked down the aisles. I had the hammer in my purse, along with my 9mm. I worried the leather strap wouldn't be able to take the weight.

We found the hammers about halfway down the center aisle, hung on pegs by their business end. I checked the bottoms of the handles and found price tags identical in shape to the traces on the hammer used in the attack at my house.

After spending another couple of minutes wandering around and trying to look inconspicuous, we went up to the counter, where I put on my best Sweet Little Old Lady face.

"Excuse me. I wonder if you could help me. I hired a couple of men to put in window boxes for my flowers, but they made a horrible mess and left the job undone. I'm afraid I made the mistake of paying them before they finished, and now I don't think they'll come back."

The man looked sympathetic. "I'm sorry to hear that, ma'am. You should always hire a licensed contractor. I can give you a list of local ones if you like."

"Oh, that would be lovely. But you see, my son is in an awful state about it, and he says he wants to take legal action. I think that's a lot of bother, but he says I should find out who these men were."

"You don't have their names?"

"Um, no. Silly me, I forgot."

"Oh, I see. Did they give you a business card?"

"Yes, but now I can't find it."

"Can you tell me what these two men looked like?"

Whoops. I couldn't exactly say they were wearing ski masks and carrying lethal weapons.

"Well, I can't exactly remember. They were young, but everyone looks young after you get to a certain age. Both quite tall and strong."

The man blinked. "Can you remember anything else?"

"No, I'm afraid not."

"I see."

He didn't look surprised by my vagueness. One of the annoying things about getting old is that everyone begins to underestimate you. Of course, that can come in handy at times. It doesn't stop it from being annoying, though.

He turned to Liz. "Did you see these men?"

"No, I just help her drive."

The man nodded. "That's very kind of you."

I can drive myself, thank you very much!

"I was hoping you might know them," I said, pulling the hammer from my purse. "You see, they left this, and I was wondering if they bought this in your shop. It looks almost new."

He took it and turned it over in his hands. Then he looked at the bottom and the fragment of a price tag still attached.

"Oh, yes. This is from us, and now I know the people you're talking about. Never seen them around here before. Two fellows in their thirties or so. One with sandy hair and blue eyes, the other Italian-looking with brown eyes and curly black hair."

I suppose.

"That's right. I remember now!"

"Well, I don't think they gave their names, but I do remember them. They bought a whole load of stuff. Drills, wiring, a soldering iron, a bunch of fertilizer, you name it. Ran up a big bill. Felt like I could close early, they paid so much. And I think I know where your son can find them. The fellows paid in cash, had a big wad of it, and when the Italian one opened up his wallet, a card from Home Is Where the Heart Is popped out."

I was familiar with Home Is Where the Heart Is thanks to my son, who is in the real estate business. It's a collection of short-term rental properties on the north side of town.

I also knew why their business card popped out

of the hitman's wallet. It's a heart-shaped card made of plastic that has some device in it that makes it beat like a real heart, complete with soft heartbeat sounds. It's as creepy as it is impractical. One year Martin went to Halloween as a Heart Man. He managed to scrounge dozens of these cards and pasted them all over his body. The effect was terrifying.

As he talked, I kept looking around. There was something off about this hardware store. I noticed Liz checking it out too.

"So they're living there," I said. "I suspected they were out-of-towners. They didn't seem to know about the Tick Tock Café when I mentioned it, or any of the other local places."

"Yes, you always want to hire a local, ma'am." He opened a drawer and pulled out a sheet of paper. "Here's a list of certified carpenters who can help you with your window box problem. Do you need any other work done? I have lists for plumbers, electricians, air condition installers..."

"Oh, that's quite all right, thank you," I said, taking the list. "And thank you so much for the information. Perhaps my son can track them down and get my money back."

"I hope so, ma'am. I don't like seeing people get cheated."

The bell jangled over the door. A middle-aged man in overalls came in wearing a John Deere cap.

"Hey there, Clyde," the hardware store owner said. "I'm just finishing up with these ladies, and I'll be right with you."

"That's all right," Clyde said. "Just need to pick up a box of nails and some engine grease."

Clyde walked down the far aisle. We watched him go. There was something strange about him too.

We thanked the hardware store owner and left.

"Strange place," Liz muttered as we closed the door behind us.

"Yeah," I said, frowning. "It was different somehow. The people were different too. Not sure how, though. I can't put my finger on it."

"Cheerville Hardware. Weird name."

I stopped, suddenly figuring it out. "No, it isn't. It's a perfectly ordinary name."

Liz's eyes lit up. "Yeah, it wasn't called Hard Up Hardware or Walk the Plank: Woodworking Supplies For Pirates."

"And the people working and shopping there were ordinary too."

"Nobody was walking around on stilts or wearing a three-piece suit made of balloons."

I shook my head. "I really expected more out of this place. They're not even trying."

"This town's going downhill," Liz grumbled.

We got back in the car.

"If they know my house, they'll know this car," I said. "How are we going to scout out those rental properties?"

"Not sure. But we better act fast. I think I know what those wires, soldering iron, and fertilizer are for."

"Something that will make your wedding go out with a bang?"

Liz nodded grimly.

"Yes." I sighed. "I'm afraid you're right."

"Let's rent a car," Liz said. "I'll pay. Do you know a place?"

I had a naughty idea. A grin spread across my face with enough cheekiness to rival Martin's at his cheekiest.

"Yes, I know just the place."

Hot Rod's Hot Rods was Cheerville's car rental agency for local showoffs. If you wanted to rent a gold-plated Mercedes for your bachelor party, this was the place to do it. If you wanted to impress your date by pulling up in a Lamborghini, you could find one here. If you wanted to do your supermarket shopping in a Bugatti, Hot Rod had you covered.

I had never been here, only knew about it because Frederick had rented a Ferrari 288 for his high school reunion.

Yes, a Ferrari 288. That kind of dates him. He really wanted one when he was in high school, and the closest he could come was to rent one to show off to a bunch of aging school friends.

He's successful enough he could buy one now, but he's more practical than when he was a teen. It's hard to imagine when you're raising a teen, but they do get practical one day. People grow up, get serious, and focus on the important things in life.

Well, most people.

Hot Rod was not one of those people.

You could tell that right away.

Amid a lot of gleaming, powerful vehicles expertly designed for speed and elegance, Hot Rod stood out like a peacock among warthogs. Yes, I should be comparing a peacock to another bird, but no bird is as ugly as a warthog, and if warthogs had wings, they'd definitely be the ugliest bird.

And Rod, to get back to my point, was a peacock.

From what I'd heard, Hot Rod had always been called Hot Rod. He had turned heads since high school, had been voted Most Likely To Break a Supermodel's Heart, and surprised everyone by not moving to the big city to pursue whatever career impossibly good-looking people pursue.

Instead, he became Cheerville's most successful salesman.

Hot Rod's Hot Rods was hugely successful. It was a local tradition to rent an impossibly expensive car for the least excuse. Birthdays, weddings, christenings, monthly haircuts, a drive in the country, no event was too important or too trivial not to tempt Cheervillians from coming to visit Hot Rod and leave with one of his hot rods. I suspected everyone was just using it as an excuse to see him.

I understood why. He was stunningly attractive. I first noticed him walking down Main Street one day, and I turned to my daughter-in-law and said, "Oh my, Hot Rod really is as handsome as they say."

I didn't even have to ask her if that was Hot Rod. It was statistically impossible for there to be two people in the same town who were that stunning.

And now I was seeing Hot Rod for the second time, strutting through his lot of luxury cars as gleaming and high-class as the best of them. He wore a loose shirt unbuttoned except for the bottom two buttons to expose a perfect chest, a belt buckle in the shape of a pair of golden lips, and jeans so tight they'd make a nudist blush.

As a matter of fact, Liz *was* blushing.

"Oh. My. God," she whispered.

"Never seen him before?"

"No," she squeaked.

"Perhaps you should try to convert him to the naturist lifestyle."

"It gives me a heart condition just thinking about it."

Hot Rod strutted up to us. "Hey, lovely ladies, how can I get your motor running today?"

"You already have," I replied. "And I thought I was all out of gas."

He snapped his fingers and pointed at me, making pistols out of his hands.

"Wrongo, my sexy senior citizen. You're never too old to pop your clutch and roll. Do you drive stick?"

Liz sputtered.

"One should never leave one's transmission on automatic, young man," I replied.

"Old school. I like your style. Come this way, my gray-haired goddess, and I will put you in the driver's seat, Hot Rod style."

I thought Liz was going to have a conniption.

You'd think having a hobby that involved getting naked with a large crowd of strangers would make her a bit more blasé. She handled the gunfight better than this.

Hot Rod showed us around a variety of fine machines, us trailing him, taking care not to get in one another's view.

At last I settled on a Lamborghini. Well, settled isn't the right word. One doesn't "settle" on a two-hundred-fifty-thousand-dollar car.

I rented it for three days at a rather steep price, most of it insurance, and settled into the ergonomic driver's seat.

Hot Rod stood to one side. He gave me a smoldering look. Decades shed off my age in an instant.

"You look like you're fast. Are you fast, girl?"

I tried to give him a sultry smile. It's been a while since I tried that on someone.

"I can be as fast as you want me to be, Hot Rod."

He pumped a fist in the air. "Make that hot rod hot, baby!"

I hit the gas, tore out of the lot, and screeched down the highway access road, shooting up the on-ramp and into the fast lane, making a hundred in two point six seconds.

Liz looked back at the sign for the rental agency, which featured (what else?) a photo of Hot Rod.

"That's the Cheerville I know," she said.

"Big time," I replied.

"I don't think that hardware store is going to stay in business for long."

"Maybe as a novelty."

"No one is going to recognize us in this. It's flashy and everyone will stare, but no one will think it's us in here. Good idea getting tinted windows."

"One can't be too careful with hired assassins."

"Speaking from experience?"

"Little old me? Nonsense."

As we shot down the highway at one hundred ten miles per hour toward the Home Is Where the Heart Is development on the north side of town, wondering what we'd find once we got there, Liz asked the other big question looming in my mind.

And like the first question, I had no answer for her.

EIGHT

"So if this wedding actually does come off, who are you going to bring?" Liz asked.

Liz had told me that since not many of her or her husband's people would be able to make it, I could bring two friends rather than the usual one.

"I really have no idea," I admitted. "Maybe I should bring Hot Rod."

"Keep dreaming. No, seriously."

"I don't know. Maybe Martin, my grandson. I already mentioned it to him. He's fourteen. Will there be other kids there?"

"Rick has a couple of nephews about that age who are coming. They can sit in the back row, texting and gaming."

"Texting and gaming through your big day?"

"Better than groaning and moaning. And they'll like the tanks and all the food. But don't you want to bring Octavian?"

I winced. My boyfriend would be the obvious choice. Sociable and pleasant, he would be great company for me and all the other guests, but it felt a bit awkward asking him. We'd been dating for more than a year now and getting closer. We even went on a cruise together. I cared for him. No, cross that out. I loved him.

And that made me feel terribly guilty. James and I had discussed the possibility of our deaths on numerous occasions. It's only natural when you get shot at for a living. We had promised each other that if one of us got killed, the other would go on with their life, that we wouldn't get stuck in mourning and end up lonely.

We promised that and meant it. But promising and doing can be two different things.

Especially when James didn't die in the field, but from natural causes shortly after both of us retired.

It felt like such a cheat and made it doubly hard to go on with my life.

If James had died in the field, I would have been devastated, of course, but I would have been mentally prepared. I would have grieved, bucked up, and soldiered on.

But finishing all the missions, surviving all the ambushes, dodging all the bullets (at least most of them), only to have James die in a hospital bed, that really blindsided me. When we retired, we both let out a big sigh of relief and looked forward to many long, uneventful years together.

It didn't turn out that way.

So now here I was, a widow solving murders in a sleepy town with a ridiculously high death rate, trying to sort out my feelings about Octavian. Finding him was a godsend, but the whole thing was tinged with guilt about James, a guilt my wonderful dead husband wouldn't want me to feel.

And yet I did feel it.

Taking him to a wedding would make me feel it more. And it might send a signal I didn't want to send.

Or at least I didn't think I wanted to send. Or didn't want to admit to myself I wanted to send. Or didn't want that signal rejected, whether or not I wanted to send it or not.

That last bit was definitely true. I wasn't sure about the rest.

Firstly, we had to stay alive until Liz's wedding

day. If these mystery men managed to kill us, my confusion over wedding plans would quickly become irrelevant.

And thanks to the ultra-expensive machine I was driving, we were already coming up on the Home Is Where the Heart Is development.

I eased off the gas, put it in lower gear, and growled down the off-ramp. All thoughts about James and Octavian and what to do with the remaining years of my life got set aside. We had a mission to accomplish. That had to be the focus.

Home Is Where the Heart Is was a small development about a mile away from the freeway, tucked in a forested area a little outside of town. A planned community, it had a single road accessing it, which passed under an arch with a big beating heart at the top. How they got a five-foot-wide heart to beat, I didn't know. I didn't want to know. I just wanted to keep Liz's and my hearts beating. There were a couple of guys living here who felt otherwise. Maybe more.

The road took us into a little maze of lanes lined with identical little houses with postage-stamp yards and little fenced-in back gardens. I'd heard that these houses could be rented by the day, week, or month, and were popular with visiting businesspeople and new arrivals. Many of Frederick's clients stayed here as they set up their new homes.

Being the middle of a weekday, it was pretty quiet. Few cars were in the driveways, and we saw only a young woman pushing a stroller and an older man washing his car. Good. Fewer people to get caught in any potential crossfire.

"How are we going to find them?" Liz asked. "All these houses look the same."

"No idea. I doubt they're making their fertilizer bomb on their front lawn."

"We should have asked what kind of vehicle they were driving. Keep an eye out for out-of-town plates."

"These are short-term rentals. Lots of people are going to have out-of-town plates."

"Good point." She scanned the street as we drove slowly along, the powerful engine rumbling in protest at being so underused.

We did a loop and started to come back along the same way. That made me nervous. While we were anonymous, we were conspicuous. These guys might get edgy if they noticed the same car kept circling around.

"There!" I cried, pointing.

I hadn't noticed the first time around, but there was a bit of fertilizer spilled on one of the empty driveways. One of the bags must have burst when they took it out of their car.

"Sloppy," Liz said.

I nodded. Very sloppy. I couldn't understand these guys. They had some good gear and intel—a silencer, knowledge of our movements, the know-how to make a fertilizer bomb—and yet they were amateurish at the same time. Trying to attack us with a hammer. Renting a boat where the police would know where to look. Not cleaning up after themselves.

It didn't make any sense.

"We should go check out their house while they're not around," Liz said.

"Assuming they're not around. There's at least two of them."

I got to the end of the street and turned, the house disappearing from sight.

"True. And they might come back at any minute," Liz said, her hand straying to the holster under her vest.

"Of course, we could call the Cheerville Police Department and let the authorities handle it," I said.

We looked at each other for a moment then burst out laughing.

"Yeah, bad idea," I admitted. "They'd only muck it up. Besides, Police Chief Grimal would ask questions we couldn't answer."

"We could tell him, but then we'd have to kill him."

Hmm. There's a thought.

"Let's ditch this rolling call for attention and walk over there," I said.

"All right."

We headed back out the gate and drove a couple hundred yards until a turn in the road hid the car from view of the development entrance, and I parked on the shoulder.

We got out and started walking away from the car as quickly as possible, both of us knowing without having to mention it that we had to disassociate ourselves from the car, otherwise it would be useless as camouflage later on.

"Hey!" came a call behind us.

So much for that plan.

We turned and saw a boy of about twelve cycling toward us.

"Is that your Lambo?" he asked.

"A friend's," I replied.

"It's cool."

"Thank you. Shouldn't you be in school?"

The boy shrugged. "I'm having a sick day. Can you give me a ride?"

"Didn't your parents tell you not to accept rides from strangers?"

He gave me a look like I was an idiot. "That's for strange men. Women aren't dangerous."

Liz and I burst out laughing for the second time in five minutes. She really was great company.

"Go on home before I call the truant officer," I told him.

His look went from disdainful to confused. "What's a truant officer?"

"I don't think they have them anymore," Liz said.

"That explains a lot," I replied.

We kept walking. The kid followed us on his bike. "Can I have a ride? Please? I won't tell anyone."

"Do you live here?" I asked, pointing to the development we were planning on sneaking around in if we could get rid of our pesky little follower.

"No."

"Maybe you should go home then."

"Why? It's boring at home. Where are you going?"

"To, um, visit some friends."

"Why don't you drive there?"

I turned on him. He stopped.

"If I give you five dollars, will you go away?"

His face brightened. "Sure!"

I paid him off, and he cycled away, no doubt to the nearest dispensary of refined sugar.

"I hope you don't do that with your grandson," Liz said.

"My grandson is much better behaved. He doesn't interfere when my life is on the line."

We passed through the gate, the giant heart thudding above us. I wondered if the people in the nearest houses lost sleep with that thing.

Walking along the sidewalk in full view of the street and houses made me feel terribly exposed, but I didn't see any other option. I supposed we could have hopped over the fences of several backyards to come up on them from behind, but that would have made us even more conspicuous, and I wasn't up to it anymore. My back was holding out thanks to Bubba Chong, and I didn't want to risk messing it up again.

The woman with the stroller passed us on the other side of the street. Luckily, she was chattering away with her baby and didn't take any notice of us.

As we passed her, Liz said in a low voice, "Besides my pistol, I have a pen knife. I can probably pop the door open. Most residential doors are pretty weak, and with the right twist you can rip right through the doorjamb."

My, my, she was full of interesting information. Of course, I knew that, too, but I was a former CIA agent.

"I have a set of lock picks in my purse," I told her.

"How interesting. I never got to learn how to use those. My work was a bit more... assertive."

"You got quite assertive in my living room. Thank you for saving me and my acupuncturist."

"Thank you for saving me while I was saving you. Here we are."

The best way to remain unnoticed is to act like you belong someplace. Liz had obviously learned the same thing because we didn't skip a beat as we walked right up to the front door. There was a heart-shaped welcome mat, of course.

"If one of them is here, we're in big trouble," I said.

"No, he's in trouble. Give me your purse. I'll pretend to search through it for the keys and shield your hands from view as you pick the lock."

"Spoken like a true pro."

"I was only a forward observer."

"And I was a kindergarten teacher."

As Liz shielded me with her body and fumbled around my purse like she was looking for keys, I got to work on the top and bottom locks. They were a common type of lock, and it took less than three minutes.

I was slipping. I used to be able to do that in under one minute. I guess I was out of practice. Picking locks on the doors of hired assassins was not how I had planned to spend my retirement, but I couldn't complain. It's a good way to keep the brain sharp.

The door opened, and my heart did a little flippy-flop as I wondered if I'd get a bullet in the next instant.

I did not. We faced a hallway leading to the kitchen in back. Stairs led up to the second floor. To the right, an open doorway led to a living room.

Quickly we shut the door behind us and drew our guns. Just because we didn't get plugged the instant we crossed the threshold didn't mean there wasn't a bad guy lurking in here somewhere.

We checked out the living room and saw a furnished-yet-sparse room like most rental properties seemed to have. In the half light of the sunlight shining through the drawn white curtains, we saw nothing of note there except a welcome letter and a half-empty gift basket of fruit and chocolates. I picked up the letter.

"Welcome to Home Is Where the Heart Is! We provide the best short-term accommodation Cheerville has to offer! If there's anything we can do to make your stay more comfortable, call us toll-free at 1-800-55HEART."

The date on the letter was from three days before.

So they'd been here awhile, scouting out the situation. They obviously hadn't known where Liz lived at first, or they would have hit her at a better time than when they did. The question remained—how did they know she'd be at the lake at that particular time?

And how had they found my house? They must have trailed me, and we didn't notice.

That was no small feat. I'm trained to spot things like that. So we were dealing with professionals.

Professionals who came only partially equipped and occasionally made basic mistakes. It didn't make any sense.

Liz was already moving past the sofa and coffee

table through a doorway, leading with her gun. I followed.

We found ourselves in the dining room and with plenty of interesting things to see.

But just at that moment, the honk of a car horn outside made us jump.

NINE

Liz and I froze, ears cocked for any sound from within the house. The honk repeated. Was one of the hitmen summoning another one who was here in the house? Maybe alerting him to our presence?

A pro wouldn't do that. He'd sneak up on us. But these guys didn't always act like pros.

That made them unpredictable and potentially more dangerous.

No sounds came from within the house. Did that mean no one else was here, or he was sneaking up on us?

We tiptoed back into the living room.

The car horn honked again, just outside the house. I gritted my teeth.

Liz moved to the doorway, whipping low around

the corner to cover the stairway and hall to the kitchen. Her every movement showed her to be a pro. I eased over to the window. The curtain was drawn just past the edge of the glass, and by angling my head I could see through a thin slice of the window.

I couldn't see much, just the front of a car on the street. It was stopped in the middle of the narrow lane.

There was another honk, followed by a shout.

"Move!"

"No, you move!"

"You're on the wrong side of the street!"

"No, you're on the wrong side of the street!"

Two horns honked at once.

I opened the curtain a little.

Two cars were stopped facing one another a couple of feet apart. They were both in the middle of the street. Both drivers were leaning out of their windows, shouting at each other.

"You're in the wrong lane!"

"No, you're in the wrong lane!"

Shaking my head, I dropped the curtain back into place and signaled to Liz, who joined me.

"What's going on?" she whispered.

"Cheerville."

She shrugged, and we moved back to the dining room to look at what had caught our attention before we got distracted by the two idiots outside.

The dining room table was covered with gear—a soldering iron, bits of wire, metal shavings, several empty boxes of nails, and clumps of fertilizer.

While we had suspected they were building a bomb when we heard about their purchases at Cheerville Hardware, seeing the actual evidence gave me the chills. I glanced at Liz. She looked pale. Imagine planning for your wedding and discovering that someone wants to blow it up!

The honking outside continued. She frowned.

"Shall I shoot them?"

"A tempting prospect, but it might attract unwanted attention."

"Let's search the rest of the house."

The kitchen had nothing of note, and so we crept upstairs to the sound of continued honking. We were now all but certain we were alone in the house. The way these guys acted, one of them would have burst outside with a hammer and smashed the cars into scrap metal.

Upstairs we found two bedrooms and a bathroom. The bathroom had nothing of note except the wastebasket, which had the wrappers for a few bandages. That made me smile. At least we left our mark on them. The bedrooms had very little. Each had one small suitcase in the closet and a few unremarkable clothes. On the top shelf were their ski masks and other black clothing. Wherever they were at the moment, they weren't going to make a hit on anyone.

We began to search more thoroughly, rifling through drawers and peeking under mattresses. Learning how to search a room while leaving it precisely as you found it is a skill that has to be learned, and Liz had learned it. We each took a bedroom and went through the place with quick efficiency. Time was ticking, and we had no idea when those two thugs would get back.

"Bingo," Liz called from the other room.

I hurried over. Tucked under the bottom of a lamp was a piece of notepaper with a typed series of letters. They were bunched into groups from three to eight letters, but were gibberish. Obviously a code.

"I know someone who can crack this," I said. I still had lots of contacts at the CIA. The folks at the Decryption Department would be happy to help.

"Good." Liz pulled out her phone and took a photo of the page. "Maybe we can finally learn what's going on."

We searched for a few minutes more as the honking continued outside and found nothing else of note.

That was significant, actually. We found no weapons, no receipts or store bags showing where they might have come from, no labels that might have told us their names. Nothing.

We also didn't find the fertilizer bomb.

"Time to go," I said.

Liz looked around uncertainly. "Maybe we should we wait here and ambush them?"

"We could, but I'd like to find out where they took that bomb. It could already be set up, and if we ambush them, we might end up having to kill them. Even if we capture them, they might not tell us. They're erratic but seem determined."

"How quickly can your friends decode that message?" Liz asked.

"Depends on how elaborate a code it is. I'll get them right on it once we get to safety."

I peeked out the window. Those two fools were still in the middle of the road, honking at each other. Several people had come out of their houses to stare.

"They're drawing too much attention," I said. "Let's sneak out the back."

"All right."

We headed downstairs. I relocked the front door locks so our mysterious friends wouldn't know we'd been there and moved to the kitchen, where a back door led to a small backyard of grass with a heart-shaped flower bed in the center.

The fence wasn't too high and led to the backyard of an identical home that faced the next street. Nobody seemed to be home, but we couldn't be sure. We'd just have to take that chance.

Liz helped me over the fence, my back giving me a twinge of protest, then hopped over it herself. I winced as the top of the board snapped under her weight.

We stared at the board missing a good eight inches off its top.

"They're going to notice that," I said.

"Sorry."

"If you hadn't been bearing most of my weight when I climbed over, I would have been the one to snap it."

We tried to fit the broken piece back on the top, giving me a recollection of my grandson trying the same thing when he smashed his skateboard into his parents' fence. We got equally unconvincing results.

"Nothing we can do," I said. "Let's get out of here."

We hurried across the backyard, passing its own heart-shaped flower bed. In satellite imagery, this neighborhood must have looked like an organ donor bank.

Our luck held, and we passed out the garden gate without anyone screaming at us like we were the burglars we technically were.

After that, we walked quickly down the street back to the car, the sound of persistent honking fading in the background behind us.

Roaring down the highway at one hundred ten miles per hour, we discussed our next move.

"I'll send this photo of the code to my friends. I'll need to get home and use my computer, though," I said.

"Why not use your phone?"

"It isn't secure."

"Neither is your home."

"Good point. No other options, though. Unless you want to let me use your secure computer." I gave her a sly smile.

She avoided my gaze and looked out the window. "Can't."

"That's what I thought."

As I hoped, there was no sign of the intruders when we returned to my house. We passed it twice and didn't spot anyone, then parked the Lamborghini down the street so no one would associate us with it.

We burst into my home like the intruders had earlier that day, although with more professionalism and better weaponry. Other than scaring Dandelion from her spot on the armchair to bolt back under the sofa, it accomplished nothing. They weren't here.

A quick check of my house revealed they hadn't been back to search it. Good. If they found out too much about me, that might lead them to my son, Frederick, and his family.

With Liz standing guard in the other room, I accessed the private CIA server, sort of like the untraceable Tor network but with even more robust security. You could see all sorts of dark corners of the Internet via this server with complete safety. More importantly, you could send emails to your colleagues in the CIA without any foreign agencies hacking them or being able to trace you. I looked up the Decryption Department and sent them an urgent request. Yes, despite being retired I could still send urgent requests to the CIA. James and I did a lot for them back in the day, and the organization has a long memory.

Just as I finished sending the email, a volcanic rumbling emerged from my laptop, increasing in strength so much that I had to turn the volume down. Martin was making a video call.

Martin had made me install an app called BOOM. ("Tired of boring old video chat apps? Tired of looking at your friends in the same old rectangles? Get some BOOM into your life!") It was a video chat app with a teenage twist.

I opened the dialog box, and my screen was filled with a video of a nuclear explosion. The giant mushroom cloud filled the screen in brilliant color as a guitar played a blaring heavy metal riff. As the guitar reached a crescendo, backed by thudding drums, the video switched to trees waving in a red hurricane, buses being knocked over by the blast front, and a long shot of the mushroom cloud rising high into the sky.

I recognized the footage. It was from a 1953 test at the Nevada Test Site of the atomic cannon. It was a giant artillery piece with a two-hundred-eighty-millimeter bore, capable of launching a fifteen-kiloton shell a distance of seven miles.

Yeah, I know my retro atomic weapons. I'm a geek that way.

And yes, they really developed an atomic cannon. Cold War thinking at its dumbest. Hey, at least they didn't invent an atomic hand grenade.

As the picture zoomed in on the fallout, the music suddenly cut out, and the picture was replaced by the face of my teenaged grandson, all buckteeth, blond hair, and smiles.

"Hey, Grandma! What do you think of the new intro?"

"Very old school. I didn't think kids listened to metal anymore."

"Only goths and emos. It makes good theme music for gaming and video calls, though."

"You are a constant educational experience for me."

"So am I really going to this wedding?" he asked as his image disappeared and our avatars starting running through a desert landscape. I hurried to put my fingers to the keyboard so I could shoot the terrorists about to pop up.

"Only if you want to. Liz says there will be other kids there."

"Oh, okay," he shouted over the sound of his M16 blasting apart a terrorist. I chucked a grenade at an approaching enemy Hummer and blew it into a flaming wreck.

"Do you have some nice clothes to wear? INCOMING!"

We ducked as an enemy RPG flew right above us

and blew a hole in a nearby wall. My health bar went down to thirty percent, thanks to the shrapnel.

"Wow, Grandma, you really get into this game. You shouted that like a real soldier."

"Force of habit," I mumbled.

"What?" my grandson asked over the sound of gunfire.

"So do you have a suit or something?"

"Grandpa Octavian says I should wear a tux."

I froze. Grandpa Octavian? When did he become Grandpa Octavian?

I knew Octavian had been spending a bit of time with Martin, taking him to ball games and that sort of thing. The poor little guy was growing up with only one grandparent—my daughter-in-law's people lived on the other side of the country—and so he loved having another older adult to spoil him.

You might think that Octavian was doing this to get in good with me, but he didn't have to, and he knew it. No, he was trying to get in good with my son Frederick, who was not at all happy to see his dear departed father getting replaced. Frederick had never been rude to Octavian—he is a difficult man to dislike—but their interactions had always been awkward.

Frederick hadn't minded Octavian spending

time with Martin, however. My son knew that Martin needed some older people in his life. It's only natural. An "Uncle Octavian" would have been welcome.

But a "Grandpa Octavian"? I doubted Martin called him that within earshot of my son.

For the first time, I realized what this increasing friendship between Octavian and Martin meant. If he was "Grandpa" and I was "Grandma" then...

"Whoa! Got you!"

Martin's words snapped me out of my thoughts. My avatar lay dead.

"You have to pay attention to what's going on around you, Grandma," Martin chided.

Yes, it's called situational awareness. I'm good at that in the field. Not so much in my personal life.

"Oh dear. Terrorists are such a bother."

"I'll put it on an easier mode." Suddenly we were in a bunker in the middle of the woods as zombies shuffled toward our position. I started blasting them apart with a pump-action shotgun.

"Whoa, headshot! Nice one, Grandma."

"I never feel guilty about killing dead people."

"Like you ever killed anyone! So are you asking Grandpa Octavian?"

"We'll see."

"Mom and Dad are too busy. Who else are you going to ask?"

"I do have friends, you know. Liz is a friend."

Martin gave me a cheeky grin. "Isn't she already going to the wedding?"

"I certainly hope so. Look, Grandma is a bit busy right now. How about I call you tomorrow?"

"Come on, let's kill more zombies."

"I really need to go."

"Okay, only fifty more zombies."

"Ten."

"Twenty."

"All right."

Parenting is all about bargaining. I've learned that grandparenting is much the same.

We killed the zombies, and I said goodbye. Then I hurried around the house, filling Dandelion's bowl and packing an overnight bag. Neither of our houses were safe. Just as I finished packing, a ping from my computer brought me back to the screen.

It was an email from the Decryption Department, saying it looked like a pretty simple code they should be able to break within twelve hours.

Well, that was a relief.

I cleared the cache on my hard drive, turned off

the computer, and stood. As I lifted up my bag, my back gave another twinge.

Great. Some bad news to follow the good. It was just like being back in the field. Good news never lasted long without something coming along and ruining it.

I hoped my back could hold out until all this was over.

TEN

Liz said she knew a good hotel on the Interstate, so I followed her directions just past the city limits, where we took an off-ramp.

"I didn't see a sign for a hotel."

"It's the kind of hotel you only find on the Internet."

"Um..."

We shot down a narrow county road with nothing but forest on either side. Then the land to the right cleared, and past an open field I saw a neon sign announcing the Assignation Inn. The sign was of a woman's face that flickered between a smile and a wink then a hushing finger to the lips.

"Is there something you want to tell me, Liz?"

"It's not what you think." She snickered.

"I can't imagine how it could be anything but what I think."

The building appeared ahead. It was a one-story structure built like a motel, where you park right in front of your room. The only lights were at the front, where a sign said Reception.

"Well, they certainly won't think to look for us here," I said.

I'm not a prude. I think I've mentioned that before. Perhaps I've mentioned it too often and come off as prudish. But I'm not prudish. Really.

It's just that I felt very, very uncomfortable driving up to reception in this sort of place.

The reception desk was actually a drive-through window like you get in fast food restaurants. I drove up, noticing there were no security cameras like in every other hotel I've ever been to. In fact, there was a little sign under the window saying, "There are no cameras on the premises. This is a surveillance-free zone. Long live privacy!"

I was surprised every burglar in the state wasn't here breaking into the rooms.

The man behind the window was an older fellow with an unconvincing comb-over. Of course, all comb-overs are unconvincing—balding men should simply embrace this particular sign of aging and cut their hair short—but his comb-over was especially so. He had a massive bald spot running from where his hairline must have been when Nixon was president to well behind his ears. Only a narrow fringe remained, which he had grown to Rastafarian length in order to sweep across his shiny pate, where it made a U-turn and came back for another pass. He must have spent a fortune on hairspray.

"Good evening. Welcome to the Assignation Inn. What kind of room would you like?"

He didn't look at me when he spoke.

"One with two beds, please."

Surprisingly, this request didn't surprise him, but his response surprised me.

"There's a surcharge for more than five people in a room."

I blushed then said, "It will only be the two of us."

That got me blushing even more.

"By the hour or for the full night?"

More blushing. "The full night."

He still wasn't looking at me. Then it struck me —he was blind. So literally no one was going to see us coming into this place. It was a cheater's heaven.

"What kind of beds do you want? We have waterbeds, Magic Fingers beds, beds with mirrors on the cei—"

"Normal beds. Beds to sleep in. Oh, wait. You have Magic Fingers?"

The man smiled. "Just like the good old days."

"We'll take those."

"Jacuzzi?"

"No."

"Steam room?"

"No."

"Video studio?"

"No!"

"That will be seventy-five dollars, please. Checkout is at 11 a.m."

I paid in cash. He put the money through a counting machine.

He passed a room key and two towels through the window.

"Room six. Have a nice time."

I drove around the hotel until I found room six, Liz snickering all the way. I have to admit I was cross with her. We had had a conversation about her nudism, and I had made it clear that I didn't want her baring all around me. She had accepted that.

Now she led me to this place, which I felt was a breach of our agreement.

On our side of the motel, only two other cars were parked. As we pulled up in front of our room, a middle-aged couple came out of their room, looking ashamed, got in their car, and quickly drove away.

Shaking my head, I went up to our door. The doormat said Home Sweet Home. An odd choice.

The room was even odder. It was a midsized room with two twin beds, a large television, and red plush carpet. The walls were adorned with paintings of churches, weddings, and men holding babies. Yes, men holding babies. Remember those pictures that were really popular in the nineties of hunks holding infants? Ever wonder where they all went? The Assignation Inn is your answer.

"I don't think these people thought through their target audience when picking the décor," I said.

"Oh, yes they did," Liz said, putting down her bag, locking the door, and checking her gun.

"At least there's a good bed," I said, checking the mattress. It was clean, thankfully, and nice and firm. No creaking. Thank God for small miracles.

Speaking of God, the Gideon's Bible on the bedside table sat on top of the table instead of in the drawer where it usually goes. The same with Liz's bedside table. There were also several pamphlets on relationship counseling. The previous tenant had a weird sense of humor.

I examined the room. I'm not picky about rooms. Hiding out for three weeks in the slums of San Salvador got me accustomed to less than one-star accommodations, but I didn't want to touch anything nasty left over from the previous occupants.

To my surprise, everything looked immaculately clean. Too bad I didn't have a black light. Or perhaps that was a good thing. I read an article on a travel blog once where a young man, braver than I, had gone into a cheap motel with a handheld black light. The stains from certain, um, substances that are invisible to the naked eye will show up under a black light. What that poor travel writer discovered was more horrifying than the slasher movies Martin thinks I don't know he downloads.

Curious, I went into the bathroom to find it equally clean. On the sink were two glasses labeled "His" and "Hers."

"This is a strange place," I muttered, moving back to my bed. Right next to the headboard was the coin slot for the Magic Fingers, something I hadn't used in years. I didn't even know they still existed.

I plunked a coin in the Magic Fingers, eased

myself into the bed with a few twinges, and lay down as the mattress started to vibrate.

"Ahhhh," I said. "Who needs an illicit love affair when you have Magic Fingers?"

The bed sent soothing vibrations through my back, easing the knot along the spine and spreading a sense of relaxation through my entire body.

That relaxation got abruptly canceled when Liz picked up the TV remote.

"I don't want to see anything this TV has on it!"

Liz laughed. "Don't worry."

A Christian network came on. Liz started flipping the channels, passing through sermons of various Protestant preachers, Catholic bishops, rabbis, even a Muslim imam. Then she came to a variety of those family channels where everyone is squeaky clean, nobody swears, and all problems are easily solved. If only.

"What gives?" I said. "It's like they're trying to drive cheating couples away."

Liz turned off the TV with a triumphant smile. "They are. This motel was set up by my church, Cheerville Methodist. It's a trap. We get cheating couples to come here with an alluring website, then guilt trip them right back to their families."

"I thought you were crazy for bringing me here. Now I see there's a Methodist to your madness."

"No puns. I'm a gun owner."

"So am I. Pity we'll never get in a gunfight with each other. I wonder who would win," I said, lying back on the bed and plunking another coin in the Magic Fingers.

"It would be interesting," Liz agreed. "But let's save our fighting for the guys who've been trying to kill us."

"It's a deal. I promise no more puns."

"Good, because otherwise I'd have to punish you," Liz said.

"I wouldn't want that. In a fight, you're as fierce as Attila the Pun."

"I'm going to get into my punjamas and go to bed."

"Isn't that word from Punjabi?"

"I believe it is. Tomorrow let's get breakfast at a bakery I know. It's not far from here and has excellent hot crossed puns."

"Stop puntificating and go to bed."

"All right." Liz switched off the light. I got changed, put another coin in the Magic Fingers to buy enough time to drift off, and climbed into bed.

"I just hope my friends can crack the code," I said as the Magic Fingers lulled me to sleep.

The next morning, they did.

ELEVEN

I was back at my secure home computer. We had approached my house as carefully as the night before and found no evidence that our unwelcome guests had been there in our absence. My guess was that they had been monitoring the neighborhood and saw I hadn't come back. My car was tucked in the back lot of Hot Rod's Hot Rods, and I felt sure they had correctly surmised that I had spent the night elsewhere.

They couldn't have guessed where I had actually stayed, or that I had gotten a restful sleep thanks to the Magic Fingers. Not quite as good as Mr. Chong, but it will do in a pinch.

"I got it!" I called out to Liz, who was dividing her time between peeking out the windows and trying to coax Dandelion out from under the sofa. The fight had left her seriously spooked.

My cat, not my friend. I don't think anything could spook Liz.

"That's great! I presume I can't come in there while you're on whatever page you're on. Can you print it out for me?"

Asked like a true professional. "I'm doing that right now, and I won't look at it."

"Thank you."

"It's only professional courtesy."

"I'm just a forward observer."

"I'm Marie Antoinette."

I pulled the page from the printer, folded it to conceal the writing, and walked out to hand it to her. As she took it away to read in another room, my phone rang. Octavian. My boyfriend. Courteous, sweet, and refreshingly normal. The only shot he's ever heard fired in anger was on the evening news.

Well, at least until meeting me and getting kidnapped. But that's another story.

"Hey, pretty lady!"

"Hello, Octavian." Hearing his voice was just as good as getting treated by Magic Fingers.

"Would you like to get a coffee this morning? How about somewhere other than the Tick Tock

Café? I'm tired of having to stop the conversation every fifteen minutes."

"Oh, I'm afraid I can't today. I'm helping a friend with a few things."

I hadn't told Octavian that Liz was getting married and I was invited because that would bring up the obvious question of who I would bring as a guest. I still hadn't answered that question. Granted, I was a bit distracted at the moment, but even if I wasn't getting attacked by unknown assassins, I think it still would have been a long, difficult decision.

Octavian paused a second. "That's all right. Oh, you know that organic delivery place, Eat Your Vegetables or No Dessert? I just subscribed and received an amazing box of fresh vegetables. The only problem is, it's far too much for me to eat myself, and if I don't eat it all, I don't get a coupon for two free sundaes at We All Scream for Ice Cream. Martin and I wouldn't want to miss that. So maybe you could help us. How about I bring over some of them and leave them on your doorstep?"

I felt a sudden surge of panic. Visions of Octavian getting gunned down on my doorstep filled my mind, his handsome face splatting into a pile of carrots and green beans like that poor wedding planner did with the cake. Even worse, I saw Grimal coming, examining the body, and then pulling out a carrot from under Octavian's head and chewing on it.

I couldn't let that happen.

"Um, no. You see, they're cleaning the street today, and it will kick up a lot of dust. I don't want them to get dirty."

"You clean your vegetables, don't you?"

"Well, sure, but…"

"Or maybe you can stop by my place while you do your errands and pick them up."

Again I had visions, this time of those hitmen trailing me like they did before, and me, Liz, and Octavian all killed in a burst of machine gun fire.

"Oh, I'm afraid that won't work either. I'm ever so busy."

"Hmm. I guess I could try to give them to the folks at the senior center."

"Perhaps you could give them to Martin?" I suggested. "Learning that he has to eat his vegetables before getting dessert might be a good lesson."

"Oh, I don't think he'd be open to that message coming from me."

"I suppose not." Silly me. Octavian's role was as mentor and spoiler, not disciplinarian. That was Frederick's and Alicia's job.

Unless...

"Does the package include cauliflower?" I asked.

"Yes."

"What about brussels sprouts?"

"Yep. Mighty good ones too."

"Perfect! Martin hates both of them. Frederick and Alicia have had a terrible time getting him to eat them."

"Well, I don't see how I'd have any better luck."

"I noticed you like spicy food. Indian and Thai, for example."

"Sure."

"Well, my son and his wife don't. They never put any seasoning in anything." They really are kind of bland, but I love them both dearly. "Martin loves spicy food. Why don't you cook up something fiery with the cauliflower and brussels sprouts and bring it over to him?"

"Hey, that's a good idea! I'll make it a challenge, tell him I don't think he could get through it all. He loves a challenge, like when he's trying new tricks with his skateboard. Thanks, Barbara. Give me a call when you get done with all your errands."

"Bye."

I hung up with a smile. What a darling. I hadn't met his children—they all lived in different states—

but I would love to. I bet they turned out very well-adjusted.

Liz must have been waiting for me to get off the phone because she entered as soon as I stopped talking. Her face was somber.

"Bad news?" I asked.

"Not as bad as it could be, but bad enough."

"Care to share with the rest of the class?"

Liz managed a smile. "As much as I can. When I was stationed in Afghanistan—"

"As a forward observer."

"As a forward observer, right. We were doing a lot of work to smash the drug trade. Burning poppy fields and breaking up distribution networks. That sort of thing."

I nodded. People often wonder why the tribes of Afghanistan are constantly warring over dusty mountains and little valleys. The answer is drugs. With no functioning government and a permissive tribal culture, Afghanistan is one of the prime producers of illegal narcotics. When I last checked, the country produced ninety percent of the world's opium and a third of the world's hashish. That is a lot of money, and it's the drug fields that the tribes are fighting over.

That and the fact that they're a warrior culture

and simply like to fight for fighting's sake. A man isn't a man unless he's got a Kalashnikov in his hand.

"So these guys are after you for disrupting the drug trade. But these aren't Afghanis," I said.

"No, they're Americans on the other end of the drug trade. Part of a cartel who got put out of business because of our work overseas."

"Good for you, except now they're out for revenge."

"Yes."

"Seems odd. Drug production wasn't destroyed in Afghanistan despite your best efforts. In fact, it's almost back to prewar levels."

Liz grimaced. "Yes, it is. That country is impossible to rule. Even Alexander the Great couldn't conquer it. That should have taught later generations something, but it didn't. The British tried and failed. The Soviets tried and failed. And now we've tried and failed. The countryside is still full of poppy and marijuana fields held by various tribes. All we managed to do was put a dent in their production and put a few of the smugglers out of business."

"So why go after a government agent? Oh, sorry, forward observer."

My joke only got a ghost of a smile.

"Revenge, as I said. The guy who runs this trade

is called Crazy Andy. Real name Andrew Weir. He's the rare drug kingpin who actually samples his own product. And not just opium and hashish, but harder laboratory-made stuff."

"So instead of sitting in front of the TV and eating Doritos, he's tweaking out?"

"It's remarkable. He graduated with honors from the chemistry graduate school at Harvard. Got started cooking up methamphetamine and acid in his home lab. Made a fortune. But there was a lot of competition at that time from bigger players. They tried to co-opt him, and when he made it clear he didn't want to work for anyone else, they tried to rub him out."

"I take it that didn't go so well."

"No. That's when he got his reputation as Crazy Andy. He set about killing members of other drug operations with a brutality that made the Mexican cartels look like followers of Gandhi. They finally made a truce, and he got a seat at the table. He also expanded his operations into the international sphere, and that included Afghanistan. While designer drugs are all the rage, there are still plenty of people who want the old-school stuff."

I bit my lip. The international war on drugs was like throwing stones against the tide. The drug barons were relentless, always coming back no matter how hard you fought against them, and their trade flowed into every corner of the world.

Even Cheerville. Even Martin's school. Oh, he'd never mentioned it, and I doubt at his age he had ever experimented, but it was there, because it was everywhere. And sooner or later he'd be made that offer. Sooner or later, he'd have to make that decision.

"So this Crazy Andy guy has gotten a fixation on you for some reason? Did you tangle with him directly?"

"Yes. He had gone to Afghanistan personally to oversee a major deal. Went to Pakistan on a tourist visa and slipped over the border."

"An easy thing to do."

The Afghani-Pakistani border had so many holes, it made Swiss cheese look watertight.

"His big meeting ended up the target of one of our raids. We grabbed the shipment, worth tens of millions, took out some of the tribesmen and some of Crazy Andy's people, and stopped the whole operation."

"But, as usual, the bigwigs got away."

"Yeah," Liz said with a sigh.

It was always the same.

"So now this lunatic wants to make an example of you."

She shrugged. "Not me personally. He wants to take out any member of our team. Make an example and send a message. I'm just the one he managed to track down first. A lot of my team members are younger and still posted overseas. I'm an easy target."

I nudged her. "Not as easy as he planned."

"Not at all," she said with a grin. "And I think I know why our murderous friends have been so unpredictable. Crazy Andy's operation took a big hit thanks to us. He had boasted about his Afghani connections and how he was bringing in a big shipment. He had to borrow a lot to get the money for it, and made a lot of promises we made him break. He nearly bankrupted himself paying everybody off and lost a big share of the drug trade. Because of this, a lot of his smarter people went off to work for other cartels, leaving him with only the druggies and crazies."

"Are you saying the people who came after us after using? That would explain why they're so erratic. When they're sober, they can plan a pretty good attack, and when they're high they mess up."

"Exactly. It explains why their planning is so slipshod too. And their lack of funding means they could only afford to buy one silencer on the black market."

"They don't even have that anymore."

"They still have that fertilizer bomb. Considering they didn't blow themselves up making it, they must have been sober when they did that."

"Which means it will work just fine when they decide to set it off. Great. So how do you think we should proceed?" I asked. This was her show, after all.

"I'm tempted to tell the police. Considering the threat level and the power you have over that police chief—"

"—for lack of a better word—"

"—they could bring in a SWAT team from some better precinct. Grab them before they do any damage and put them away for decades on terrorism charges."

"You're tempted to do that, but you're not going to do that."

She gave me a knowing grin.

"Nope. Because if we only grab the hitmen, we don't get the big guy."

"And how do we do that? Crazy Andy is probably not anywhere near Cheerville. He may not even be in the country."

"His last known location was in this region. While that intel is a year old, drug dealers tend to stay put because they have to build up local and regional networks."

"That doesn't mean he'll come running just because you want to capture him," I said.

Liz got a determined look on her face, the kind of face I'd seen on soldiers when their unit was pinned down and they'd decided to rush the machine gun nest that was trying to slaughter them.

"I think I know a way to change that," she said.

And so she told me.

While I complain of various ailments thanks to age—a trick back, occasional knee pain, having to use reading glasses, et cetera, et cetera, et cetera, I have always had a good heart.

Not after she told me.

Now I have the heart of a woman twice my age. It's not a good feeling.

TWELVE

I really, really didn't like this plan.

It was a clever plan, for sure, but it was also an insanely dangerous plan. It was bold, highly risky, but offered the opportunity of wild success.

It sounded like the kind of plan Crazy Andy might think up.

And I didn't want to be a part of anything like that.

Not that I had much choice.

"He's always gone for showy spectacles," Liz explained. "The fertilizer bomb is just his style. I bet the only reason the hitmen tried shooting me first was because they heard at the last minute where I'd be, and they didn't have the bomb ready in time."

"They saw a good opportunity and went for it, despite orders."

That made sense. Most militaries, or groups of drug-dealing thugs, allowed for their people to have some autonomy on the field. Any experienced commander knew that plans generally flew out the window as soon as the mission got underway.

"If we can tempt him with a spectacle, something that will impress the other cartels, he can get in good graces with the drug network and rebuild his empire."

I groaned, rubbing my temples. I felt a headache coming on.

"So your idea of tempting him is to allow them to kidnap you and do some video execution? And you think Crazy Andy will fly in to do it personally?"

Liz nodded. "Most of the killings he did to build up his empire he did personally. He likes it, and it made him feared. When we made him lose status, not to mention the bulk of his business and followers, he swore revenge. He's boiling with hatred for me and my team. He wouldn't pass up the chance to draw the knife across my throat personally."

I shuddered. Yes, if he wanted to get in good again with the Afghanis, that would be just the way to do it.

"So you actually want to let them kidnap you," I said. I could barely believe the words coming out of my own mouth.

"It's the best way to get Crazy Andy out of hiding."

"It's the best way to get you killed."

"He's a master at evading the law. We tried for years and were never able to track him down. When we captured some of his men, they were more terrified of him than the prospect of life in prison. And now that he's lost most of his power, the agency I worked for isn't monitoring him anymore. You know how it goes."

I do know how it goes. Every agency has limited funds, and they have to go after the big guys. The smaller operations pass under our radar.

"If he's as smart as you say, he might suspect it's a trap."

Liz smiled. "Of course he will. That's why we'll make it a trap."

"What do you mean?"

"I've been thinking. How could they know I'd be at the lakeshore right at that moment? They knew I was getting married because there was an announcement in the newspaper. I should have my head examined for doing that."

"You thought you were in civilian life again. It happens."

"Yeah," Liz said, a tone of bitterness coming into her voice. "I slipped up. And why shouldn't I? I mustered out two years ago."

She slumped, looking at her feet. I put a reassuring hand on her shoulder.

"The past has come back to take a bite at me too," I told her. "More than once. But remember that you're still part of a team, just like you were when you were on active duty."

She nodded, standing a little straighter. I bet she was a wonder in the field.

"So I'm thinking they've bugged the Lakeview Park building," she said. "The announcement in the newspaper said where we were going to get married. The building is open to the public most days, so it would be easy to plant a device. They overheard Fiona Younger talking about me coming over the other day, and they made a hasty plan to target me."

"That makes sense. Yes, I think you have it. Oh my God, Liz! I just thought of something. The schedule in the hallway. It has your wedding listed with the date and time!"

Liz paled, her jaw dropping. "The fertilizer bomb. They're going to detonate it at my wedding!"

"Not if we can help it."

Liz looked me in the eye, nodded, and said, "Let's get to work."

We sped over to the wedding venue in my hot rod. I was really getting to like this thing. Pity I couldn't afford to buy one. It would certainly impress the boys in my life. Yes, Octavian might have been in his seventies, but he was still a boy. Once a boy, always a boy. A trait about men I find equal parts irritating and endearing.

"So what's the plan?" I asked.

"I'm sure they're monitoring their bug at the Lakeview Park building. It's easy enough to do with a simple ear pod linked to the receiver. They probably take turns wearing it day and night. We'll go to the building, and I'll talk about how I'm going to change venues so we'll be safe from them. You know Woody Nook?"

"No."

Liz smiled. "Great. Then I'll have to give you directions."

We roared into the parking lot and squealed to a stop with a burn of rubber on asphalt. Only a few cars were in the parking lot. An elderly woman getting out of her old Ford gave us a frown. Many of

Cheerville's citizens didn't like any sort of ruckus. They wanted a boring, quiet town. If only.

Indeed, as we stepped out, she called over to us.

"We're having the senior knitting class. Could you keep the noise down so we can concentrate, please?"

It's amazing how the word "please" can, with the right tone, become a demand rather than a question.

"I'm terribly sorry. We'll be sure to keep quiet," I said, louder than necessary.

The woman glowered at us and stomped in. Liz and I exchanged mischievous glances. Having a younger partner was bringing me back to my rough-and-tumble youth. I had thought I'd mellowed with age. Now it appeared that the mellowness was only a veneer.

"I should get back in the Lamborghini and rev the engine," I said.

"We have work to do."

"Spoilsport."

We entered the building, which in the middle of a weekday was given over to senior citizens and stay-at-home moms. The first room we passed had a sign saying Mommy and Baby Yoga. Curious what infants looked like doing yoga, I peeked through the door's little window. Infant yoga turned out to be a circle of sleepy-eyed young women in tights sitting on yoga mats while pulling up their babies, stretching out their arms, and plopping them down again.

Playing with their kids, in other words. Well, if they wanted to sit in a circle together and call it yoga, I suppose it wasn't much harm. Having been the mother of a baby myself, I knew how desperate I was for a bit of adult company.

We moved on, passing the knitting class. Through the open door we saw a circle of women, mostly older than me, all gossiping away like mad. Their snapping voices made a perfect counterpoint to the clicking of their knitting needles. I don't know what they were all so angry about. They didn't have a small child to take care of.

Or a murder to solve.

The woman who had snapped at us in the parking lot noticed us peering in and frowned.

I gave her a smile in return.

"Enjoy your class!" I shouted.

Everyone turned and gave identical frowns. Liz chuckled and elbowed me in the ribs, and we continued down the hall.

Silently she motioned toward the main room, the

one where poor Fiona Younger had met her cakey end.

I nodded. If the bug was anywhere, it would be there.

And I had just the thing to search for it with.

A nonlinear junction detector is a handheld gadget that detects electronic devices. Bugs, for example. Perfect for police, private detectives, or senior citizens who have friends in mortal danger of being blown up.

It looks like a miniature metal detector like those crazy old men use to find pennies at beaches. My model could fold up and be stored in my purse. I used it regularly to scan my house for surveillance equipment.

We came to the room and found it empty. All the better.

"It's a pity we'll have to cancel," Liz said, "I really liked this venue."

"It does have a nice view," I replied.

I paused to look at the room a moment. The picture window had been replaced, the carpet cleaned, and the police tape was long gone. It now looked like a mostly empty function room. I wondered if some infant yoga or senior's knitting class had already been held here.

Poor Fiona Younger. Her senseless death had been erased so quickly.

She deserved justice.

"At least I can get a refund," Liz went on. "They were very understanding considering the circumstances."

"We'll get them," I replied.

Liz and I spoke in our normal voices. It's tempting when speaking with the intent of being overheard to project your voice, or be overly emphatic like a nervous actor on stage for the first time. Professionals resisted that impulse, and Liz, I had come to learn, was as much a professional as I am.

"The police are on it," Liz said. "Chief Grimal looks like he's capable, and he told me he has every available officer on the case."

It took all my professionalism not to laugh out loud.

"They'll get those two guys," I managed to say in a normal voice.

As we spoke, I pulled the nonlinear junction detector out of my purse, switched it on silent, and began to scan the room.

"So this is what I wanted to show you," Liz said. "Woody Nook is roughly the same size as this room, so we can set up much like we planned to set up here. We'll have the food table right in the middle here, with the cake taking up the center spot. The DJ is still willing to come, so we'll put him over here."

"Won't we have to keep the music down if we're outside?"

"Not a problem. North Cheerville Park is pretty spacious. But yeah, we won't be able to play any of Rick's hard rock."

"Fine by me," I replied.

My device flashed a couple of times as I swept it slowly around the room, first for a motion detector used as part of the security system at night, and again for the temperature control system. I moved to another part of the room.

"Now the seating will be a bit of a problem. I guess we'll have to find somewhere to rent some folding chairs."

"I'll look up where to do that," I said, continuing my scan.

"I guess I'll have to keep the thumb drive with me even through the wedding. Until Grimal catches them, I can't let it out of my sight."

Clever. Tempt them with something juicy.

"I can guard it if you want," I said.

"No. You're taking enough of a risk as it is.

Another problem is the photographer," Liz said. "He worked with poor Fiona a lot and heard what happened. Now he's cancelled. Says he scared."

"I have a cousin who can do it," I said as I walked slowly along one wall, scanning it.

"Is he professional?" Liz asked.

"Not really. He's good, though. I'll show you some pictures. He took some wonderful shots in Kenya last year."

We were getting really good at improvisation.

"We're still getting those tanks, at least," Liz said. "Megaton Army Surplus isn't scared of anything."

"Maybe we can load them with live ammo. They can act as security."

"We won't need it. I won't even tell the guests about Woody Nook until that morning."

"Good idea."

I stopped. The scanner was flashing. In front of me was a light fixture, a bowl of frosted glass over a light bulb.

Liz spotted it, gave me a look, and strolled to a far corner to fetch a chair.

"Hopefully they'll have caught those guys by then. If not, they'll have no idea where the wedding is taking place."

She came back with the chair and set it down,

masking her movements by saying, "Woody Nook is on the park map. I'll get a bunch of them to give out to guests so they don't get lost."

Liz stood on the chair, looked in, and gave me a grim nod.

"I can go with you if you want to take a look at it," I said.

"That would be great. I'm still too scared to use my car. They must know about it."

"And you think I'm not?"

Liz let out a reasonably believable laugh. "We look silly going around in that pickup!"

Clever girl. Makes it sound like we borrowed a vehicle from a friend. Of course, she didn't say "your brother's pickup" or "your neighbor's pickup". Too obvious. We would both already know who we borrowed it from and wouldn't need to say so. She really was a pro.

And now those two thugs will be on the lookout for two ladies in a pickup instead of a Lambo with tinted windows.

"Look," I said. "I'm getting tired. We've been running around all day, and I'm still shaken by those people breaking in. Can we go up there tomorrow?"

Liz gave me an appreciative look. We needed to give Crazy Andy a chance to get into town.

"Oh, all right," Liz said, sounding convincingly annoyed. "But can we go early?"

"How about I pick you up at ten?" I suggested.

"Ten it is, then."

We stared at each other. We had just made an appointment with death.

THIRTEEN

On most missions, waiting is the worst part. Your adrenaline is up, and you can find no release. You know you'll head into danger at a certain time, and the hands on the clock seem to freeze, teasing you with an endless, sleep-depriving wait.

You learn to deal with it, but you never get used to it, and you never like it.

We had nothing to do until the next morning, and we had to keep ourselves scarce in the meantime. So we hid out in the Assignation Inn, Liz flipping through a novel, me reading the paper while plunking an endless series of coins into the Magic Fingers. Its vibration and steady buzzing relaxed me, at least a little.

We spoke little, each wrapped up in our own thoughts.

Early in the evening, my phone let out a rumble like it had suddenly transformed itself into a miniature volcano. I opened it to find the BOOM app telling me I had a video call from Martin.

Not a simple call. Teenagers don't ever seem to call unless there's video involved.

The video showed a cloud of ICBMs coming right at me. I touched them to answer.

"How did this app end up on my phone? I never installed it," I demanded when Martin's avatar appeared, buzz-cut and square jawed and armed heavily enough to take out an entire terror cell singlehanded.

"Hi, Grandma!" the shirtless and impossibly muscled Martin answered in a voice five octaves lower than Darth Vader's. "I installed it for you because you don't know how."

"I'm perfectly computer literate, thank you very much."

Martin's avatar laughed. It sounded like an avalanche. "Who should we fight right now? Terrorists, Nazis, or zombies?"

"While I'm always partial to terrorists, I'm on my

phone right now. The controls are too fiddly, and I might end up shooting you instead of the bad guys."

"Oh, are you out?" An adult would ask if this was a bad time, but Martin, being fourteen and my grandson, assumed that any time would be a good time to talk to me.

He was right, of course. Hearing his voice, even masked behind a Herculean avatar, gave me a sense of normalcy I desperately needed. It felt even more relaxing than the Magic Fingers.

Not that I would give that up. I plunked in another coin.

"Yes, I'm with a friend," I said.

My mind raced to think of a good cover story in case he asked where I was and what I was doing. He didn't. Why would that be of the least interest?

"That's cool. Well, if you can't play on that crappy old phone—"

"Language."

"—then you can watch me."

Remember what I said about adults being the perpetual audience?

The screen changed to an African jungle. Monkeys swung from vines. Tropical birds darted beneath the canopy. Radicalized locals popped out of the thick underbrush, AK-47s blasting. Martin started mowing them down.

"So is Grandpa Octavian coming to the wedding?" he asked between shots.

I blinked. "You told Octavian about the wedding?"

"Yeah, I told him a week ago when you told me."

So he knew about the wedding all this time and didn't let on just so I wouldn't feel pressured to invite him? That man understood me so well.

But of course he would. He was a widower just like I was a widow. He knew me asking him to something like that would hurt.

But perhaps it would heal as much as it would hurt.

"I haven't decided yet," I admitted.

"Why not? You said this Liz person is letting you bring two guests. If you bring me, then you can't bring both Mom and Dad. So you should bring Grandpa Octavian."

The faultless logic of a teenager who had never experienced real suffering. Bless him.

When you've traveled as much as I have, you see a lot of suffering, and you see a lot of kids who are adults before their time. Twelve-year-olds breaking rocks by the side of dusty highways. Eight-year-olds left home alone to take care of three younger siblings because both parents have to work fifteen-hour shifts at some Dickensian factory. Street kids of all ages who have no parents at all and have to scavenge and beg and steal just to keep themselves half a meal away from starvation.

Those people may have been young, but they were not children. You could see it in their eyes. They understood loss. They knew death.

Martin did not.

That innocence was what people like me fought to protect. The chance for kids to be kids in a safe and loving environment. The chance for adults to carve out a bit of happiness for themselves. While I knew it didn't always work out that way even in the First World, it did more often than it didn't, and considering the amount of chaos and evil in the world, I counted that as a victory.

And a minor miracle.

So why didn't I ask Octavian? Assuming I didn't die tomorrow, assuming Liz and I caught the bad guys and the wedding went ahead as planned, why shouldn't Martin go to his first wedding with his surrogate grandpa? And why shouldn't I enjoy Octavian's company?

James wasn't stopping me. He had urged me,

time and time again, to continue with my life if anything ever happened to him.

"You should invite Grandpa Octavian," Martin said again. He'd killed seventeen terrorists and blown up two armored vehicles, and I hadn't even replied to him.

"I will, Martin."

As soon as I said it, I felt better, like a persistent ache had eased. I smiled and put another coin in the Magic Fingers.

"Cool. It will be fun. He says weddings always have lots of food and cake and stuff. What's that buzzing noise?"

"Nothing, Martin. I need to go now."

"To call Grandpa Octavian?"

"Yes."

"Like you're going to call him right now?"

"Yes, Martin."

"Cool, bye."

He hung up midbattle.

That was how anxious he was for "Grandpa Octavian" to come along.

And that was when I realized where all this was headed. I had been worried about getting too close to Octavian, worried about getting hurt by loss again, and had been blind to the fact that he had already become an integral part of my life. Indeed, he had, in a way, already become family. Martin seemed to be the only one to have noticed that.

Liz had been quiet through all this even though with the high volume BOOM was always set at, it meant she had heard every word.

I glanced at her out of the corner of my eye. She was pretending to read. There are subtle physical clues that show if someone is pretending to do something or actually doing something. Her eyes scanned the lines of the book without actually focusing. Dead giveaway.

Putting another coin in the Magic Fingers so it wouldn't cut out while I spoke to my boyfriend, I lay back on the bed and called him.

He picked up on the first ring.

"Hey, pretty lady!"

"Hi, Octavian."

"Still busy with your friend?"

"You could say that, yes."

"I took your advice, and I'm cooking up a vegetarian vindaloo that will blow Martin's socks off."

"That's great. Just don't make him sick."

"Him? No, he's a little tough guy. I'll make him beg for mercy and drink five gallons of water, though."

I laughed. "Say, um, Octavian?"

Pause. "Yeah?"

"I was wondering if, um. You know, my friend Liz is getting married in a few days. Liz says I can bring two guests. And Martin wanted... well, I wanted you to... come too."

Longer pause. "When is it?"

Oh dear, he sounds less than enthusiastic.

Well, why wouldn't he have doubts? He lost a spouse too!

I told him the date and time then added, "There have been a few hitches, so the date isn't set in stone."

It felt almost like a relief to say that, as if I was giving him a back door to escape through.

"I'd be happy to come." Again that half-hearted tone. I heard him clear his throat. "Yes, I'd be happy to come." More decisive this time. "I'll take care of Martin and get him to the venue. I'm sure you'll be busy with Liz. Will you be busy until then?"

"Tomorrow looks to be quite eventful. I'm not sure of my schedule after that."

To put it mildly.

"I can imagine. I know how weddings sweep up everybody's time. I'll see you there if I don't see you sooner."

"Great. I'll text you the details. If anything changes at the last minute, I'll call you."

"All right." Pause. "And Barbara?"

"Yes."

"Thank you for the invitation. We'll have a great time."

I smiled. "Yes, Octavian. We will."

I hung up, put the phone on the bedside table, and lay there as the Magic Fingers performed a stand-in operation for Bubba Chong. It turned out I didn't need them. I felt far more relaxed now, having made more than an invitation, but a decision, perhaps a major life change.

I decided to go to sleep. I needed the rest. If I was going to enjoy that decision, I would have to fight for it.

FOURTEEN

Woody Nook was "what it says on the tin," as the British say. Set in the far corner of North Cheerville Park, it was a small cul-de-sac enclosed on three sides by trees. The open area measured about fifty yards by thirty, with trees and fairly thick underbrush all around that stopped us from seeing very far inside the woods. A gentle slope led down to the rest of the park, a couple hundred acres of woods, grassy expanses, and hills given over to dog walkers, joggers, and picnicking families.

On a weekday morning, we had the place to ourselves.

Good. We didn't want anyone getting caught in the crossfire.

While it felt bucolic and peaceful, Woody Nook was actually quite close to the northern parking lot, which led by a winding two-lane road to the highway and its access road. It actually would have made a good wedding venue.

It made an even better ambush point.

For them.

My trusty 9mm weighed down my purse. Those two hitmen never saw my gun, and so wouldn't suspect this nice little old lady was packing.

The problem was, those two hitmen knew Liz was armed and dangerous, so she had to look as unarmed and harmless as possible.

Which was why she wore only gym shorts and a halter top.

There was nowhere for her to hide a gun, and in fact she didn't have one at all.

That made my heart age several more years.

Of course, coming unprepared to a gunfight was all part of Liz's insane plan. Because if you obviously didn't have a gun, a gunfight might never start.

Liz was banking on them seeing a good chance to capture her and execute her in style, plus maybe find out about that mysterious thumb drive she had mentioned.

Or they might decide to go with the original plan they had at Lakeview Park and gun us down from a distance.

If they went for that option, our special backup plan would do us no good at all.

We walked up the gentle rise leading to Woody Nook. The only sound we heard was the wind blowing through the trees and the soft *swish swish* of our feet moving through the tall grass.

"This is a really bad idea," I said.

"You've said that before," Liz replied, fingering a silver chain she had around her neck, the end of which disappeared into the neckline of her halter top.

"Let me say it again. This is a really bad idea."

Liz scanned the tree line on the three sides of Woody Nook. We were entering the cul-de-sac now, willingly letting an unseen enemy flank us. That went against every rule of strategy in the books.

Not that I ever played by the book. Liz apparently didn't either.

Maybe we should.

We walked deeper into the cul-de-sac. Liz started talking about how she would set up her imaginary wedding.

She didn't get far.

"Hold it right there!"

Two masked men emerged from the woods, one in front of us and one to the left. They were dressed in the same black outfits and balaclavas as when they broke into my house. The man in front held a hunting rifle. The man to the left had a double-barreled shotgun.

They'd rearmed themselves. Easy enough to do at the local gun shop. They could only get long arms, though. Handguns have a seven-day waiting period in our state.

It didn't matter. In this terrain, they could kill us just as effectively with what they had.

"Raise your hands above your head!" the man with the rifle barked.

We did as we were told. I did not drop my purse. They hadn't asked me to, after all.

As they approached, I could see they were high again. Their movements were twitchy, exaggerated. They'd taken some sort of stimulant. Cocaine, perhaps, or speed.

That made them unpredictable, especially since they both had their fingers inside the trigger guard. Basic firearm safety is beyond your typical drug addict.

"Just keep calm," I said in as even a voice as I could muster. "We're no danger to you."

"You pepper sprayed me, you stupid old woman," the guy with the rifle said.

Actually he didn't say "woman." He said something more objectionable. Even more objectionable than being called stupid.

They stopped several paces away, well out of pepper spraying range.

The one with the shotgun gestured at Liz.

"You. Turn around."

Liz made a slow turn to show she wasn't armed. Next, Mr. Shotgun gestured at me, a jerky movement that made me cringe.

"Careful you don't set that thing off," I said.

"Shut up and empty your purse."

I'd planned for this. Slowly, with exaggerated and deliberate movements so as not to startle our fidgety captors, I unclasped my purse, unzipped it, and turned it upside down.

Pepper spray, Kleenex, makeup, my phone, my wallet, and a nail file all cascaded to the ground.

But not my gun. That was attached with Velcro to the inside lining of my purse.

"Back away," Mr. Shotgun ordered. He gestured toward Mr. Rifle, his movement so jerky I was surprised he didn't accidentally blow his head off.

We took three steps back. Mr. Rifle slung his weapon and moved forward to pick up my things.

Yes, he actually slung his rifle, putting the strap across his chest and the rifle across his back where he couldn't quickly get to it. He was that high.

Oh, and he didn't even put the safety on. There's a reason they call it "dope."

Mr. Dope (formerly Mr. Rifle) bent over to gather up my things, grabbing the pepper spray first. This was the moment. If I kicked him in the face, I could yank out my pistol, shoot Mr. Shotgun, and then level it at Mr. Dope.

But Mr. Shotgun had a bead on me. I looked in his eyes. Bloodshot, but focused. He wasn't as high as his friend. And at only five yards away, there was no way he'd miss with a shotgun. Sure, he'd get Mr. Rifle too. No great loss. I was a bit more worried about the shotgun's effect on me and Liz.

Mr. Rifle stood up, gripping the pepper spray. "I should blast this in your face, you old bag!"

"None of that," a voice behind us said. "We got more important things to do."

We turned. From the edge of the forest sauntered a young man in his late twenties, his eyes so red they practically glowed, his movements even jerkier than the other two. He wore jeans and a T-shirt for some band I'd never heard of. He had a shock of blond hair in desperate need of a comb and scissors.

I glanced at Liz. Judging by how pale she had grown, it looked like her plan had been a success.

At least so far.

"Elizabeth Danfrith, so nice to see you in something other than camo! And who's your pepper-spraying friend? Before you tell me your name, drop that purse before I have my men put a bullet in your brain."

"She emptied it, boss."

"Drop it!" he bellowed, his face turning beet red and spit flying from his mouth.

I dropped it. His two men staggered back as if he had slapped them.

Crazy Andy stalked forward, scooped up my purse, and looked inside.

He yanked the pistol out of the Velcro holder and waved it under the nose of his goons.

"Oldest trick in the book!" He turned to us and gave a theatrical shrug. "Idiots. I'm stuck working with idiots."

"We've noticed," Liz said.

"That's *your* fault," he said, stalking up to her and flicking off the safety. "You arrested my best men, scattered the rest. Now I'm stuck with a pack of losers who can't even take out a pair of women."

"You got me," Liz said. "Let my friend go."

"Yeah, right. She gets to watch while I skin you alive on camera. Then I'll skin her alive too. But first, tell me what this thumb drive is and where I can get it."

"What thumb drive?"

Crazy Andy was not the kind of person you play dumb with. But Liz wanted to play dumb, because it got a particular reaction she was expecting.

He backhanded her so hard, she staggered several feet and fell down. I rushed to her side.

Now Crazy Andy and his thugs all faced us and faced away from a particular part of the tree line.

As I cursed them and tried to help her up, Liz played like she was more injured than she was, curled into a ball, and slipped the dog whistle out from where it was hidden in the neckline of her shirt.

She gave it a silent blast and tucked it back in as I shielded her with my body.

I got her to her feet just in time to see Poofles and Doofles lope out of the forest. They ran silently. No barking, no growling, just a pair of predators on the hunt.

"Okay! Okay!" Liz shouted to cover the sound of their near-silent approach. "You win. It's government files, entrusted to me by my team. I'll give it to you if you let my friend go."

"You crazy?" Crazy Andy screamed. "I get everything I want, and then I kill you. That's how this is going to work."

He grabbed her by the neck.

Big mistake because Poofles and Doofles went straight for him.

They rushed up, the sound of their running finally alerting the two druggie gunmen, who turned and gaped, too slow to do anything as the pair of huge hounds knocked them back and leapt on their boss.

Crazy Andy went down under a mass of muscle, fur, and fangs.

Which was the worst thing that could have happened, because they ignored the two armed men standing right next to us.

Those two men shook off their initial shock. Mr. Shotgun leveled his gun. Mr. Dope scrambled to unsling his rifle.

I looked for my pistol, but it was hidden beneath

the struggling forms of the drug kingpin and two dogs.

I looked up in terror to see two barrels of a shotgun pointing at me.

FIFTEEN

"Attack!" Liz shouted, pointing at the two gunmen.

I didn't think the dogs could turn around and get them so fast, but before Mr. Shotgun had a chance to fire, one of the Dobermans slammed into him. The man yelped and let off his gun, the pellets passing harmlessly overhead.

Then he was on the ground, his shotgun flying away as he held back the dog's slavering fangs.

I have to admit I felt for the guy. I'd been in the same position. Maybe I'd send Bubba Chong to work on him in prison.

Meanwhile, Mr. Dope was showing just how much speed there was in his system by sprinting full out for the trees. One of the dogs tailed him, biting at his rear end and tearing off a hole, first in his sweatpants, followed by his underwear. Not a pretty sight, I can tell you. Poofles or Doofles (I couldn't tell them apart) then got to work on his legs.

Several times the Doberman tried to leap on him, only to miss as Mr. Dope dodged at the last minute. He could have gotten a football scholarship if he hadn't wasted his life with narcotics and crime.

I noticed he still had the rifle slung on his back, but he couldn't stop to get it, not with that beast literally nipping at his heels.

That left Crazy Andy unaccounted for. He lay on the ground, moaning, his clothes torn and covered by several bites and scratches.

My 9mm lay half underneath him.

Liz and I dove for it at the same time.

Liz got there first, which was a good thing for me because just as her fingers touched it, Crazy Andy lashed out at her with a kick that got her right in the knee. She cried out and fell.

The drug dealer fumbled for the gun, his movements still erratic, either from the drugs or the brief but brutal savaging he had just endured from the Dobermans. That gave me the chance to grab the gun at the same time.

The only problem was he was far stronger and also got his finger in the trigger guard before I did.

I jerked my head to the side. The gun barked, a bullet missing me by inches. He hauled on the gun to bring it to bear. The muzzle pointed right at my face, a dark circle of death. He pulled the trigger and got nothing but a click.

Snarling with frustration, he smacked me upside the head. I tumbled to the ground, my back twisting and sending a shot of pain all the way down my leg.

Not now!

He stood, looking triumphant. Liz was down, nursing her knee, and I clenched my teeth from the pain of the sciatica.

Crazy Andy's triumphant expression turned to worry as a distant voice shouted, "I've called the police!"

We all looked. A middle-aged lady walking her poodle stood a couple of hundred yards downhill, a phone in her hand.

"Thank you!" I shouted back. "Run!"

She took one look at Crazy Andy, who roared in frustration, and decided that was good advice. She took off like some Olympic athlete, the poodle furiously working its little legs at the end of the leash, unable to keep up the pace and ending up being dragged through the grass.

Next, Crazy Andy spotted the shotgun lying not

far off. Liz was crawling for it, favoring her good leg. He went for it.

Liz turned around and gave him a dose of my pepper spray.

"Bravo!" I shouted.

Crazy Andy was less enthusiastic. He howled, gave Liz a kick, and stumbled back.

The pain in my back began to ebb. It felt like one of those temporary tweaks, not a crippling pain.

I hoped.

Glancing at Crazy Andy's two goons, I saw they were still out of the fight. Mr. Shotgun was barely conscious, and now both dogs had gone after Mr. Dope, who had sought safety up a tree about fifty yards from us. He had lost his rifle, too, which lay at the base of the tree, guarded by the killer Dobermans.

Liz and I crawled for the shotgun.

Crazy Andy must have realized that he had lost, because he pointed at Liz, glared at her through eyes even more bloodshot than before, let out a ragged cough, and said, "This ain't over!"

"It will be soon enough," I said, almost to the shotgun.

Crazy Andy ran.

"Sic the dogs on him!" I told her, my hand finally

grasping the shotgun. I felt much better now. Nothing like the reassuring weight of a firearm to ease chronic back pain.

"I can't. If I do, that guy in the tree will grab his rifle."

Good point. I hauled myself up to a kneeling position, feeling only a few jabs of pain. Liz tried to rise and fell back down. That kick to the knee had been a nasty one.

"He's getting away!" Liz cried.

Indeed, Crazy Andy was running like he had Poofles and Doofles on his heels.

"Not for long he isn't," I said as I leveled the shotgun and aimed down the barrel.

I fired. The heavy weapon bucked against my shoulder, wrenching it painfully. It had been a long time since I'd fired a 12-gauge.

Yes, I shot a fleeing man in the back. A fleeing ruthless killer who spread drugs around the community. I had no problem with that.

I did have a problem with range. A shotgun is not good at long range, the pellets spreading out more and more the farther they go. Crazy Andy staggered, spots of red appearing in at least three places on his shirt and pants, but he kept running.

Hopped up as he was, I'd have to blast him with an elephant gun to take him down.

The other barrel had already been fired, and by the time I hunted down some spare shells on our prisoner, Crazy Andy would be long gone.

Tossing aside the gun, I got to my feet, ignored the pain that caused, and started running after him.

Well, running is a bit of a generous term.

"I'll call the police and tell them the situation!" I heard Liz shout after me.

Like that would do any good.

I didn't bother saying that out loud. I needed to save my breath.

I ran after Crazy Andy as fast as I could, but being a man half my age, with a generous head start, and buzzing on whatever chemicals he had in his system, he soon far outpaced me.

I kept running anyway, my lungs working hard and my back twinging with every step. If he got away, Liz would never be safe.

And neither would I.

Crazy Andy headed toward the parking lot hidden by a screen of trees. His car must have been one of the ones we saw when we pulled up. He had waited in the woods until his men sprang the trap.

I was getting seriously out of breath, and Crazy Andy got farther and farther ahead.

"You can't catch me, old lady!" he called over his shoulder, cackling as he disappeared into the trees.

Oh yeah? I thought. *You don't know which car I'm driving.*

But even a Lamborghini isn't enough if you don't know where to go. By the time I passed through the trees and made it to the parking lot, he was gone.

There were a few cars in the parking lot, plus a van. I suspected the van was owned by the hitmen and contained the fertilizer bomb.

Nothing I could do about that now. I got in the Lamborghini, feeling much better in its cozy ergonomic seat, and peeled out of the parking lot and onto the two-lane road that was the only way out.

There were two options for where he could have gone. This road led to both the highway and its access road running alongside it, heading out of town in one direction or into town and joining up with the business loop if you took the other direction.

Going back to town was an unlikely option, so Crazy Andy was either headed for the highway, or taking the less-used access road.

I chose the highway. Crazy Andy looked panicked, and since he didn't suspect I had a souped-up sports car, his only worry was the police. He'd want to get out of the county, and then out of the state, as soon as possible.

That left me with two problems—I didn't know for sure that he had taken that route, and I didn't know what kind of vehicle he was driving.

As I shot up the access ramp to the highway, swerving in front of a delivery truck in the slow lane and merging with the fast lane, I decided I'd go down the highway a few miles, checking out each car as I passed. If I didn't spot him, I'd get onto the access road and head back to town, cutting Crazy Andy off if he went that way.

The engine roared as I hit ninety, soon catching up to the first car I came to. The powerful engine growled as I slowed and pulled alongside. A woman stared at me, astonished, while in the back two little boys gave me a look of utter delight. I grinned, forgetting they couldn't see me through the tinted windows, and hit the gas.

A few seconds later, I caught up with the next car, driven by a man in the uniform of a popular delivery company.

Not who I wanted. I shot forward and came to the next car, driven by a woman so focused on texting that she didn't even notice I was there.

Frustrated, I hit the gas again, the roar of the engine startling the texting woman and making her swerve.

Whoops. At least she didn't crash. She'd probably have sued me, saying it was my fault I interrupted her text.

This was getting annoying. I was beginning to think I'd taken the wrong route or maybe the wrong direction. He wouldn't have headed back into town, would he?

Then I got another problem added to my generous helping of life worries. A siren wailed behind me. I checked my rearview mirror. In the distance, I saw the flashing lights of a police cruiser.

Great. Just great.

I didn't have time for a traffic ticket. I ignored them and resumed my speedup, slowdown search of all the vehicles on the highway.

I passed five more cars, all of them driven by innocent civilians, before the cruiser caught up with me.

It came right up behind, obviously as a signal for me to pull over. Through the window I could see a police officer and Police Chief Grimal. He was eating Chinese takeaway as his patrolman drove.

Good Lord. Did that man ever stop eating?

The highway was clear up ahead except for an eighteen-wheeler in the slow lane. I hit the gas and shot forward, making one hundred mph before I had even finished laughing at Grimal.

The cruiser picked up speed too. Police cars have powerful engines, but I was driving a Lamborghini, so there really was no competition.

We crested a hill and sped down the other side, Grimal gradually losing ground. Up ahead I saw three cars. I slowed for the first one. No luck. I swerved to the fast lane, gave the engine a bit of speed, caught up with the second car, slowed down alongside, and again discovered a regular citizen. The police cruiser gained on me.

The next car was a few hundred yards ahead. I gunned the engine, overtook it, and found it was, once again, a regular citizen instead of an international drug dealer and cold-blooded killer.

This highway was seriously boring!

I passed the car, the police cruiser coming up behind me a second time, and got in the slow lane. A sign said an exit was just a mile ahead. I needed to get on the access road and try to cut Crazy Andy off.

And pray he hadn't slipped away on one of the county roads leading off from the access road. If he did that, there was no way for me to find him.

As I got on the exit ramp, the police cruiser tried to cut in front of me and force me off the road. How rude. I hit the gas, got ahead of them, then clenched my teeth as I realized I was going far too fast for the curving exit ramp. I yanked on the wheel, the screech of tires filling my ears, and missed the guardrail by a millimeter.

The police car did not, and I heard a screech of metal on metal that almost shook my fillings loose.

The policeman managed to maintain control, however, and followed me right onto the access road.

I hit the gas and left him in the dust.

Not for long. Up ahead, a Lexus came in the other direction. Clear as day, I could see Crazy Andy at the wheel.

I swerved into his lane and went right for him.

His face registered confusion then lit up. I felt sure he knew I sat behind the tinted windows of that Lamborghini. His mouth spread wide in a maniacal grin, and he drove right for me.

So he wanted to play chicken, did he? No thanks, I don't play crazy games with crazy people. It's a good way to lose.

But I didn't want him to know that. I stayed the course, the Lexus rushing up at me. Just as it looked about to smash into me head-on, I flicked the steering wheel to the right and swerved past him.

I had forgotten one little detail—the police cruiser was speeding up behind me.

Oops.

In my rearview mirror I saw Crazy Andy and the cop car come right at each other. Crazy Andy forged straight ahead while the policeman swerved to avoid a head-on collision.

They clipped each other, and both cars flipped, rolling over and over again on the narrow two-lane road.

My heart clenched. Poor Grimal! Poor innocent policeman!

As much as I looked down on the local constabulary, I didn't want them dead. I swerved the Lamborghini, made a one-eighty, and drove back to the scene of the crash.

I passed the police car, which was upside down, and approached the Lexus, which had settled right side up, half off the road and half in a ditch.

Then I saw a sight that made my blood run cold.

Crazy Andy lay in the road, obviously dead. A human-sized hole was punched through the windshield of the Lexus.

I got out, heart beating fast, and started to walk

back to the police cruiser, the pain in my back forgotten in my worry for those two officers.

With a squeal of twisted metal, one of the doors opened. The policeman staggered out, followed shortly by Grimal. Other than being covered in sweet and sour sauce and rice, they appeared unhurt.

"Wha-what happened?" Grimal asked, a noodle draped over his ear and a fortune cookie stuck to his forehead.

"You wore your seat belt," I said, and gestured at the mess in the road behind me. "He didn't."

Grimal nodded. The fortune cookie fell off his forehead to crack on the pavement. It left an indentation in his forehead that I hoped would be permanent.

"I teach traffic safety in the local schools," he said.

I laughed. "Well, at least you're good for something!"

SIXTEEN

Now that the assassins were taken care of, nothing could spoil Liz's big day. A cheerful sun shone over Cheerville, the weather was warm but not hot, and Police Chief Grimal was in the newspaper as having arrested two drug dealers and taken out their leader. The bomb squad had found and defused the fertilizer bomb in the van, making this story national news.

At least that was the version we gave to the press. No mention of me or Liz, thankfully. Our agencies saw to that. Once again, it looked like he would get an award from the governor for someone else's work. So it goes.

I let that pass. I was too busy helping Liz with her camouflage wedding dress.

We were at her house, or more accurately her suburban fortress. Poofles and Doofles were locked in a back room, their growls shaking the foundations as the bridesmaids and I fussed over the dress. She had picked desert camouflage as a memory of her time in the Middle East. While it was a strange color pattern to get hitched in, I have to say it was certainly appropriate to her lifestyle. Her military lifestyle, not her nudist lifestyle. I was so glad she wasn't having a nudist wedding. I would have found something else to do, and it would have been a shame to have missed seeing Liz and Rick get married.

Megaton Army Surplus had even provided her with a bouquet of flowers native to Afghanistan. I wondered if that meant that whoever caught it would be sent overseas instead of getting married. Or perhaps would have a wedding similar to my own.

Whatever happened, I wished that woman well.

Once everything was ready, we drove over to the entrance of Lakeview Park, stopping out of sight down the street where the pink tank was parked amid a small circle of curious onlookers. Rick's tank was parked down the street in the other direction beyond the park entrance. The plan was to have them set out at the same time, meet at the gate, and drive together to the Lakeview Park activities building where the guests would await them.

It would be one heck of an entrance.

As the bridesmaids fussed with her dress and an older woman who resembled Liz bawled in the background, my friend turned to me.

"Thanks for all your help, Barbara. This wouldn't have been possible without you."

"Don't mention it," I said then lowered my voice. "Really, don't mention it. We don't want our covers blown."

"Cover for what? I'm a forward observer." She laughed and clambered onto the tank. She looked radiant in her desert camo wedding dress atop that pink metal monstrosity.

"See you at the venue!" I said as I got in my car with a wave.

I drove to the Lakeshore Park activities building with a smile on my face. In most of the murders I've solved here in Cheerville, I've taken down individual killers, not major drug dealers with many deaths on their hands. It was a refreshing change, one that made me feel young again.

And that got me thinking. While everyone looked at me as old, seventy-one wasn't that far gone, no matter what my back said. I still had a lot of life left in me. I needed to appreciate what I had and enjoy it, not live in the past. James himself had told me many times to move on with my life in case something happened to him.

Of course, that's easier said than done. Now it had been a few years. The pain of his passing had eased to a dull ache that would never go away but that I could live with, and I had a whole new life here in Cheerville. I needed to live it more.

I parked, got out, and scanned the small crowd of wedding guests. I recognized no one. That's always a bit awkward.

Strolling through the crowd, exchanging uncertain smiles with various strangers, I waited for the festivities to begin. A waiter passed through with a tray of champagne glasses. I took one. I had earned it.

A couple of sips and the twinges in my back eased. Not as good as Magic Fingers, and nothing compared to Bubba Chong, but hey, I was at a wedding.

I drained the champagne and got a second glass to hold.

Feeling much better, I gazed out over the beautiful park.

A familiar car pulled up in the parking lot. My heart did a little flippy-flop.

Octavian and Martin got out, dressed in identical tuxedos.

"Martin, you look like a little gentleman!" I cried as I walked over.

He strutted around a little. "I look pretty cool, don't I, Grandma? Like James Bond or something."

"Definitely. Be careful not to spill anything on that."

"It's insured," Octavian said. "All kids' tuxedo rentals require that you buy insurance."

"Smart," I agreed. "And you certainly look good too."

I pulled closer to him.

"And you look very fine in that dress, pretty lady. I hope your dance card isn't full yet because I'd like to reserve a twirl around the dance floor."

I looked him in the eye.

"My dance card is entirely full and only with your name."

His eyes sparkled.

"What's a dance card?" Martin asked.

"In old-style dances, many different men would ask ladies to dance, and you kept a dance card to know who to dance with next," I told him.

"Sounds lame." Martin looked around, then his eyes lit up. "Cool!"

We turned and saw a pair of tanks rumbling over the hill, one with pink camouflage and one with blue. On the turret of the blue one sat a handsome, square-jawed young man in dress uniform. Marching on either side of the tank were more men in dress uniform, no doubt his closest Army pals, along with a few civilians in suits.

Next to the blue tank rumbled the pink one. Sitting on top was Liz in her camouflage wedding dress. Flanking her tank came the bridesmaids in much more traditional attire and the women from her family.

"Whoa!" Martin said. "They're totally trashing the lawn."

I winced as I saw Martin was right. The tank tracks were chewing up the grass, leaving a horribly mutilated twin path of destruction. Martin cheered.

Oh well, no wedding ever goes off without a hitch.

Octavian laughed. "Looks like I made it just in time."

I put my hand in his. "Yes, Octavian, yes you did."

He looked at me, glanced back at the wedding party, then looked at me again.

He moved in for a kiss, but stopped when Martin started making puking sounds. We squeezed each other's hands instead and went back to watching the pair of his and hers tanks tear up the park because we would have time later to kiss in private.

ABOUT THE AUTHOR

Harper Lin is a *USA TODAY* bestselling cozy mystery author. When she's not reading or writing mysteries, she loves going to yoga classes, hiking, and baking with her family and friends.

For a complete list of her books by series, visit her website.

www.HarperLin.com